"Fate would have it, you'd be the robbery division's first female detective."

Sam flashed her a grin, clearly amused by the situation. "Think you're up to it, McIntyre?"

He was saying that to goad her, she thought. To make her stop focusing on the uncomfortable aspect of this situation and just view it as a challenge. Appreciating the intent, she had to give him his due. "You're not as dumb as you look, Wyatt."

The comment made him laugh. "Bet you say that to all the guys."

"Only the ones who deserve it."

"You know, McIntyre, this might be the beginning of a beautiful friendship."

"Too late for that. I already know you," she reminded him.

Dear Reader,

Welcome back to another installment of the Cavanaugh saga. Riley McIntyre's story actually began in the last Cavanaugh book when her partner, Diego Sanchez, was slaughtered by the so-called vampire slayer. The death hit her hard and the ordinarily outgoing, happy-go-lucky Riley withdrew into herself. Detective Sam Wyatt is a charismatic ladies' man with his own set of problems. An affair that ended abruptly seven years ago comes back to haunt him in the form of a daughter he never knew he had. The girl is delivered to him because her mother was killed in a car accident and Sam is the little girl's only relative. With no idea how to handle a pint-size female, he turns to Riley for help. In the end, they help each other. She shows him how to be a family man, and he shows her how to get back into the game of life, big-time.

I hope you enjoy this latest Cavanaugh tale. I thank you for reading it and, above all else, I wish you someone to love who loves you back.

Love,

Marie Ferrarella

MARIE FERRARELLA

In Bed with the Badge

Silhouette®

Romantic

SUSPENSE

SILHOUETTE BOOKS
®

ISBN-13: 978-0-373-27666-0

Recycling programs
for this product may
not exist in your area.

IN BED WITH THE BADGE

Copyright © 2010 by Marie Rydzynski-Ferrarella

Books by Marie Ferrarella

MARIE FERRARELLA

This *USA TODAY* bestselling and RITA® Award-winning author has written almost two hundred novels for Silhouette Books, some under the name Marie Nicole. Her romances are beloved by fans worldwide. Visit her Web site at www.marieferrarella.com.

To
Sam Warren,
for lending me
his first name.
Hope you like this.

Chapter 1

"I'm worried about her, Brian." Lila Cavanaugh's eyes met her husband's in the long mirror that hung over the double, ice-blue-tiled sink in their bathroom. "She's never behaved like this before." They both hurried to get ready, to arrive at work early for completely different reasons.

Brian Cavanaugh, the Aurora Police Department's Chief of Detectives and, technically, Lila's superior, at least at the precinct, didn't have to ask his wife who *she* was, despite the fact that Lila's declaration had come out of the blue.

Lila referred to her younger daughter, Riley McIntyre.

Riley, like her three siblings as well as her mother, was a detective on the police force and ultimately under Brian Cavanaugh's command. Until a couple of months ago, the twenty-eight-year-old had been a happy-go-lucky, outgoing and upbeat young woman who greeted every morning with a grin and a wisecrack. Her deep blue eyes always sparkled. If Brian were to single out the stepchild with the most optimistic, positive view of life, it would have been Riley.

But the recent murder of her new partner, Detective Diego Sanchez, by the very serial killer that she and the rest of the homicide task force were pursuing at the time, had changed all that. Riley had become quiet, introspective and, at times, just plain unreachable.

It concerned him, as well.

In a way, she reminded him of his niece, Rayne, the youngest of his older brother, Andrew's, children. Right after her mother had disappeared and was presumed dead, Rayne began to act out, getting in trouble with the police despite the fact that Andrew was Aurora's Chief of Police at the time. Fortunately, Rayne had straightened out over time and made them all proud.

Granted, Riley wasn't acting out, but there was no denying that she was dealing with an excessive amount of emotional turmoil.

Was the change in her behavior permanent or temporary?

"She keeps saying she's all right, but I know she's not," Lila insisted. She gave up the pretense of applying her makeup and turned to face her husband. "I don't want her on the street like that, Brian. Being out there is hard enough when you're at the top of your game, let alone being off the way she seems to be these days." Lila hated asking for favors, even from her own husband, but this was for her daughter. "As her superior, can't you order her to take some time off until she's her old self again?"

Lila had long since accepted and made peace with the fact that her children had all followed her late husband and her into the police force. She did her best not to worry about them too much. But this new turn of events had thrown the balance off and she sincerely feared for Riley's well-being, not to mention her life.

"I could," Brian allowed slowly. His eyes met Lila's. "But I won't."

Disappointment sliced through her clear down to the bone. She had counted on his agreeing with her. "But Brian—"

"Lila, put yourself in Riley's place. When you were shot and almost died on me all those years ago, how did you feel, having all that time to think about what'd happened?" He deliberately made no reference to how he'd felt, watching her sink to the ground, or what had gone through his mind as his own hands tried to stop the bleeding, to desperately keep her life from flowing out of her body.

Her mouth turned grim. "Awful," Lila finally conceded.

And she had continued to feel that way long after she'd recuperated from her gunshot wound. Ben McIntyre, her first husband, had used the shooting to manipulate her. Jealous of what he thought was her relationship with Brian, her partner at the time, Ben had forced her to quit the force in order to become a full-time wife and mother. While she loved her children, she hated being away from the life that gave hers such meaning.

Giving up the force made her feel like only half a person.

"What I can do," Brian said, "is make Riley's status contingent on seeing the department's therapist."

"Hoolihan?" Even as she said the man's name, Lila shook her head. Her frown further underscored her disapproval.

Brian thought of himself as a fair man and he was always willing to listen to an opposing point of view. Turning around to face his wife, he leaned a hip against the sink and crossed his arms before his still rather buff chest.

"Okay, what's wrong with Hoolihan?" Brian asked.

After she'd been shot and before Ben had forced her to resign from the force, she'd seen the therapist on her own. She remembered it being a less-than-rewarding experience.

"Well, for one thing, I doubt if anyone but a robot could relate to the man." The session—and the man's cold, dead eyes—had left a bad taste in her mouth that existed to this day. "He's impersonal, removed and, frankly, the man gives me the creeps."

Brian thought it over for a moment. His own encounters with the therapist were limited to run-ins in the hall and an exchange of nods. He was in no position to champion the man.

"All right, we'll find someone else for Riley. That'll be your assignment," he said affectionately, punctuating the declaration with a quick kiss to her temple.

The corners of Lila's mouth lifted as she fisted one

hand at her hip. "And what'll you be doing while I'm searching for a sympathetic ear for Riley?"

"You mean what'll I be doing aside from the massive task of directing the detectives of all the departments?" he deadpanned. He thought of the reason he was going in so early. "I'll be making the final decision regarding finding our daughter a new partner."

Lila smiled. She liked his reference to Riley as "our daughter" despite the fact that their combined families consisted of eight adult children and he could have just as easily divided the two factions into "your kids" and "my kids." Instead, they became "ours." That was just the Cavanaugh way and it was only one of the many reasons why she loved this man so much.

"Do you have anyone in mind?" Lila asked, curious.

He looked back into the mirror to make sure he'd shaved evenly. "Yes, I have someone very definite in mind."

"Do I get a name, or do I have to guess?" she asked.

Brian looked away from the mirror. There was a glimmer in his eyes. "Depends on what you're willing to trade for the information," he teased.

Lila glanced at her watch. "We're both due at the precinct in half an hour," she pointed out.

Wide shoulders rose and fell in a pseudo-careless shrug. "Lots of things can be accomplished in a small amount of time, Mrs. Cavanaugh," he told her just as he began to skim his lips lightly along her neck.

He could make her heart race so easily, Lila thought.

She doubted if she would ever get used to this. Or take it for granted.

"So, we're skipping breakfast," she said with minor difficultly as he stole her breath away.

"Not always the most important meal of the day," he told her, slowly working his way around her throat. He lifted up her chin with the tip of his finger to expose more of the targeted area.

Lila gave up the pretense of leaving the house on time. She wove her arms around her husband's neck.

"Consider it skipped," she breathed, giving in to temptation.

"But I didn't put in for a transfer," Riley protested, stunned.

She was sitting in her stepfather's office. That morning she'd found a message on her desk saying that the Chief of Detectives wanted to see her. She'd come knowing that this had to be something official because if it was anything else, Brian would have picked up the telephone and called her at home to discuss it.

But she'd never expected to be hit with this.

"I know you didn't." Brian's voice was kind, but firm. "I decided to do it for you."

Riley had never been big on change, especially not now. "I've been assigned to Homicide ever since I made detective." A feeling of desperation began to sink hooks into her. She did her best to bank down the feeling. "Have I done something wrong? Because if I have, just tell me what it is and I'll—"

Brian cut her off. "No, nothing. You haven't done anything wrong, Riley," he emphasized. "You're an asset to the force and, most likely, this is only a temporary assignment. Robbery is currently shorthanded." He paused for a moment before adding, "And you need a change."

He saw her shoulders stiffen, as if his words had been a physical blow.

"I just need to get back in the saddle," Riley insisted.

"You never got out of the saddle, Riley," Brian contradicted. "You didn't take any time off after Sanchez was killed, even when I encouraged you. And I understand that. You're one of those people who needs to be busy in order to deal with something unpleasant that's bothering you." He smiled at her. "You're not all that different than I am in this respect," he acknowledged. Getting out of his chair and from behind his desk, he drew closer to her. "This isn't punishment, Riley. This is taking a breather, getting a change of pace—and doing me a favor," he added for good measure, hoping that would help her.

Riley took a breath. This was the man who had brightened her mother's world a thousandfold. The man who had always been more of a father to her and her brothers and sister than her own father had been. Brian was doing what he thought was best for her, but she didn't want to give up her routine, didn't want to be away from people she was accustomed to working with. This was *not* the time for her to build new relationships.

Still, when he put it like that, it was hard turning the Chief down—even though she knew what was really behind his so-called request. And "favors" had nothing to do with it.

Sighing, she realized she had no choice but to relent. Riley nodded. "All right, if it's really that important, I guess I can work in the robbery division—but just until you get someone else to fill the position."

"Thank you. I knew I could count on you," he told her. She noticed that he didn't agree with her about the temporariness of the situation. Instead, he seemed to be waiting a beat, then continued. "And there's something else."

She *knew* it. Riley looked at her stepfather warily. "What?"

"Nothing major," he assured her. "I want you to see a therapist."

Riley closed her eyes, searching for strength. "Oh, God, Chief, not Hoolihan."

"No," he agreed with a laugh, "not Hoolihan. Your mother already made that case for you," he explained when she eyed him curiously.

"Mother?" Riley repeated quietly.

So they were both conspiring against her, she thought, feeling more alone than ever. She loved them both, but didn't they understand that she'd deal with this on her own terms? In her own way? That it was just going to take her time to forget the image of Diego, lying in the alley, in a pool of his own blood, a stake driven through his heart like some character in a grade B horror movie?

This wasn't a head cold she was trying to get over

but a huge case of guilt. She should have been watching his back.

Brian nodded. "She made me see that talking to Hoolihan wasn't going to help. Your mother suggested that you find someone in private practice to help you deal with this."

Riley squared her shoulders in a defensive movement that, at one time or another, he'd seen his own four kids make. "But I am dealing with this."

Brian knew that he could successfully argue the case, but he merely said, "Humor me."

Riley sighed. She was stuck.

"How long do I have to find this 'shrink'?" She couldn't get herself to even say the word "therapist." Acknowledging the word would be like admitting that she needed help and she didn't. She just needed time, that was all.

"I would have preferred yesterday," Brian told her honestly, "but let's just say you need to find one by the end of the week."

She was definitely not looking forward to the search. "Yes, sir."

"Good, that's what I like to hear. Now, about your new partner—temporary partner," he threw in when he saw her grip the armrests and rise in her seat.

Sitting back down, Riley continued gripping the armrests as if ready to rip them out. "I don't need a partner," she protested with feeling. "I can work on my own."

"That's not how this operates, Riley, and you know it. The only time a detective goes solo is if his—or her—partner calls in sick for the day. We work in teams, Riley, we always have," he reminded her. "Homicide, Robbery, Vice, it doesn't matter what department, the procedure is the same."

Because he was a man she respected as well as loved, she decided to be honest with him, to bare her soul for the moment. "Chief, if something happens to my partner right now, I don't think I'm up to handling that."

"Which is why I said you need to see a therapist," Brian reminded her gently.

"Besides," a deep voice behind Riley said, "nothing's going to happen to me, although I'm touched that you're concerned."

Intent on making her point with the Chief, Riley hadn't heard anyone behind her. The voice, coming out of the blue the way it did, nearly made her jump. At the same time, she realized that it sounded vaguely familiar.

Riley twisted around in her chair just in time to see Detective Sam Wyatt stride in, then lean his long, muscular frame against the doorjamb. He'd filled out some since she'd last seen him.

"Morning, Chief," Sam said, nodding at Brian. "You sent for me?"

"Always know how to make an entrance, don't you, Detective Wyatt?" Brian said with a shake of his head. He gestured to the chair beside Riley. "Sit down," he instructed.

"Yes, sir." He deposited his body into the vacant chair, sparing Riley a nod. "And as for making an entrance, in this case, I had to, sir. I sneaked up on

McIntyre once and nearly wound up getting a .22 right to the chest." Sam flashed a wide, two-thousand-watt smile known to melt women at three hundred feet. "Still as fast on the draw as you were?" he asked Riley.

She wasn't the kind to boast, but something about his tone made her say, "Faster," without hesitation.

Not one to leave anything to chance, Brian made it a point to know as much as possible about the detectives under his command. He'd discovered a while back that Sam Wyatt and Riley had been friendly rivals coming up together at the academy. The thirty-two-year-old Wyatt was a bit of a charmer and there was no denying that he was flamboyant, but the man was still a fine detective and could be relied on to keep an eye on Riley until she was back in fighting form. To him, the two detectives made perfect partners—they would keep each other on their toes.

He'd gotten excellent feedback about Wyatt from Joe Barker, Wyatt's lieutenant and, as it happened, the detective's partner had just transferred back east to be near his ailing father. Wyatt needed a new partner.

And so did Riley.

"Well, since you two know each other, I'll leave it to you, Wyatt, to help McIntyre here get up to speed."

A sense of uneasiness wove its way through Riley. She really didn't want to switch departments right now. Ordinarily, she wasn't one to expect personal favors, but this one time, she fervently hoped that the chief's connection to both her mother and her would tip the scales in her favor.

Riley leaned forward in her chair. Blocking out Wyatt and focusing only on the chief, she asked, "Is this really necessary?"

"Yes, this is really necessary," Brian assured her.

Riley suppressed a sigh. There would be no winning today. "Yes, sir."

"All right, you're dismissed," he told them. Riley rose, as did Sam. She was about to leave the office when Brian said, "And Riley—"

She stopped and looked at her stepfather over her shoulder, hoping that he'd had second thoughts about this. "Yes, sir?"

"I want that name by the end of the week."

The therapist. In light of this new development, she'd almost forgotten about finding one for herself. There was no joy in Mudville tonight, she thought. "Yes, sir."

"What name?" Wyatt asked her as they walked out of the chief's office.

"Nothing that concerns you," she told him tersely.

Sam shrugged, taking her retort in stride. "Okay, but you'd better hustle."

Riley stopped walking and looked at her new, "temporary" partner. What was he talking about? "And why should I do that?"

"Because the end of the week's just three days away," he informed her simply, "and the chief likes things to reach his desk in the beginning of the day, not at the end of it."

Just who did Wyatt think he was, telling her things

about her own stepfather? Did he think she lived in a closet?

"You don't have to explain the chief to me," she retorted, annoyed, walking away from Sam.

"Right, he's your stepfather." He held his hands up as if surrendering. "I know, I know." Sam dropped his hands to his sides again as he increased his stride to keep up with her. Did she think this was a race? "I also know that him being your stepfather doesn't ultimately make any difference in the game plan. The chief's a fair man like that." The smile on his lips spread. "But there I go again, preaching to the choir. You'd already know that, too, wouldn't you?"

Give me strength, she prayed. "This arrangement is just temporary, you know."

"I know," he said cheerfully. "Until I get a better offer." Riley gave him a dirty glance. "Was I supposed to say until you get a better offer?" he asked innocently. And then he grinned again. "Sorry, didn't mean to hurt your feelings, McIntyre."

Reaching the elevator, she punched the up button. "I don't remember you being this annoying in the academy," she said.

Reaching over her, Sam pressed the down button. The look he gave her said that she'd made a mistake. Robbery was on the second floor. Homicide was located a floor above them. But she wasn't part of Homicide anymore. "Funny," he said, "I was just about to say the same about you."

Her temper flared. "Look—"

The elevator arrived. Stepping to the side to allow Riley to get on first, Sam followed and then pressed the button for the second floor.

"Hey, I get it. You feel like you've just had the rug pulled out from under you. Losing a partner can really do that to you," he agreed sympathetically. "But the only way you're going to land on your feet is to get over it and move on. I did," he told her. "Now stop feeling sorry for yourself and get on with your life—or the chief will leave you in Robbery—with me as your wet nurse."

Chapter 2

The fact that Wyatt could even *say* he thought of himself in those terms—as her *wet nurse*—made Riley's ordinarily subdued temper flare to dangerous new heights.

Since when did she need a babysitter, for pity's sake?

Was that what the chief thought, that she needed to be watched over? Worse, was that what her stepfather had intimated to Wyatt when he'd proposed the pairing to the smug, grinning hyena of a detective?

The idea sent a sick chill up and down her spine. She struggled not to shiver.

As for the other comparison he'd just made, well, Wyatt was way off base. That he even thought they were comparable showed just how little he understood. The man obviously had no instincts or feelings.

"Your partner transferred to another state," Riley told him through gritted teeth. "Mine was killed—murdered," she emphasized. "It's so far from being the same thing that it absolutely takes my breath away."

The thought of taking her breath away briefly flashed through Wyatt's mind. Not the way she implied, but the more standard, sensual way.

It was not without its appeal.

But Sam knew Riley McIntyre well enough to understand that it wasn't safe to tease her about that, at least, not right now. So instead, he took the easier route and just explained his reasoning.

"They're both gone."

"And you and mules both breathe, but that doesn't make you the same thing," she countered, then added a bit tartly, "despite the obvious resemblance."

If she expected him to take offense or announce that this partnership wasn't going to work, she was disappointed. Her words appeared to bounce right off him like rain off the freshly waxed hood of an automobile.

"Nice to know you're as sweet tempered as ever."

"Only with people who bring it out of me," she shot back, her mouth curving in a smile she definitely didn't feel.

The elevator stopped on the second floor and slowly opened its doors. Sam stepped out, then waited for her to do the same.

"Well, just a word to the wise—or in your case, wise ass," he said glibly. "Lt. Barker likes his detectives quiet—unless they're talking about an ongoing case."

She stopped walking and stared at him. "You're kidding, right?"

His face was deadly sober as he asked, "Do I look like I'm kidding?"

She couldn't tell if he was pulling her leg. She vaguely remembered that he had an outlandish sense of humor back in the day, but there was no glimmer of it right now. Or so it appeared.

"With you," she told him, "it was always hard to tell."

"Well, I'm not." He shoved his hands into his pockets as he resumed walking down the hall to the squad room. "Barker likes two things, hard workers and cases cleared. Personally," he confided, "I think Evans came up with that story about his ailing father because he couldn't take the lieutenant anymore."

"Evans," she repeated, rolling the last name over in her head. It wasn't really familiar. "That would be your partner?"

"Ex-partner," Wyatt corrected, then nodded. "Give the little lady a prize."

She stopped walking again. "Wyatt?"

Something in her tone told him to be on his guard. He had no idea what was coming. "Yeah?"

"You call me a 'little lady' again and an irreplaceable part of your anatomy will be handed to you so fast you won't know what hit you." She delivered her warning with an angelic smile.

"Yep," he murmured more to himself than to her, "every bit as charming now as you were back then."

Working with Riley McIntyre was going to be a challenge, he thought.

Once they arrived at the squad room, Sam pulled open the door for her, wondering as he did so if she would find the act of courtesy offensive on some militant-female level. But he wasn't about to make any apologies for the way he'd been raised.

"C'mon," he coaxed. "Might as well let Barker see what he's in for."

Bracing herself, Riley walked into the eerily quiet squad room.

The faces were different, the disorder was the same, she noted. Files haphazardly piled on desks and on top of computer towers. More than one stack threatened to fall at any second, waiting for the right passing vibration to send it cascading to the floor.

Organized chaos was the way she liked to think of it and she was as big an offender as anyone. Riley found she couldn't think clearly if the top of her desk was visible or her files were aligned neatly. When things were all spread out across her desk, her mind felt more opened, more prone to working fast.

Walking with Wyatt to the back of the room and Barker's office, Riley nodded at several familiar faces as she passed. The police community was a close-knit bunch and most detectives knew one another by sight, if not by reputation.

The latter was a communal one as far as she and her siblings went. At least, it had been, through no fault of their own. For a while there, all four of them were thought of as the offspring of an undercover agent gone bad.

But that was before Brian Cavanaugh had married her mother. Once vows were exchanged and it was clear that the Chief of Detectives considered Lila's children his own, the talk had abruptly stopped. Almost everyone liked the chief and those who didn't still respected and/or feared the man.

Chief of Detectives Brian Cavanaugh, younger brother of the former Chief of Police Andrew Cavanaugh, was known as a fair man who firmly believed in speaking softly and carrying a big stick. Not only carrying it but, on occasion, using that stick judiciously. The upshot of the situation was that no one wanted to get on the Chief of D's wrong side. Careers were known to have faded in that darkened area.

Seeing the way the detectives responded to his new partner, Sam commented, "I guess I won't have to introduce you to anyone."

"You can if you want to," she told him. "If it makes you feel useful, I wouldn't dream of depriving you."

Wyatt made an unintelligible noise she let pass rather than ask him to repeat himself. Instinctively, she knew it would be better all around that way.

Riley had never felt nervous meeting new people or even new superiors. But she felt something icy—a premonition?—slide down her spine as she looked through the glass wall that comprised Barker's office and saw the man sitting at his desk.

The word "trouble" ricocheted through her brain, refusing to fade away.

Sam knocked once then waited for the lieutenant to beckon him forward.

The latter, Riley noted, seemed oblivious to the knock. Either that, or he was deaf. If it was neither, then Barker was deliberately taking his time, keeping his eyes on the keyboard as he typed something. Finally, just as she was about to suggest to Wyatt that they come back later for an official introduction, Barker raised his intense dark brown eyes to silently regard the newest addition to his squad room.

An ex-marine, Lieutenant Joseph Barker looked every inch the part. From his close-cropped, salt-and-pepper hair, to his unsmiling demeanor, he was military through and through. She could almost feel the man's eyes wash over her, moving slowly as if he were conducting some kind of minute inventory.

"Take a seat, McIntyre," he finally said in a voice devoid of emotion. It certainly couldn't be termed as friendly. As Sam moved to join her, Barker stopped him before he could sit down in the second chair. "Not you, Wyatt. If I'd wanted you to sit, I would have said so, wouldn't I?"

The question was like a sharp poke in the ribs, meant to make the other detective retreat.

"Sorry, Lieutenant, don't know what came over me." The sarcastic response was delivered with an open, innocent smile.

Riley's respect for her new partner began to take form as she waited to see the lieutenant's reaction.

The look that Barker shot Wyatt was dark, bordering on black. Sam left without another word being exchanged between the two men.

Rather than say anything to Riley, the lieutenant resumed what he was working on.

Three more minutes passed before Barker looked up again.

Finally, Riley thought.

Hands loosely clasped in her lap, aware that on some level she represented her stepfather, Riley offered the man behind the desk an encouraging smile.

His first words to her were not what she would have expected.

"I heard you let your partner get killed."

Riley felt as if an arrow had been shot from a crossbow straight into her chest. Barker couldn't have said anything to make her feel worse if he'd deliberately tried. Maybe he had.

Squaring her shoulders, Riley lifted her chin and replied, "I wasn't with him at the time. Detective Sanchez went out on his own, without telling anyone."

Barker's eyes bored into her. As uncomfortable as it was, she refused to look away.

"He was your *partner,* McIntyre," the lieutenant emphasized. "You're always supposed to have your partner's back. Or didn't they teach you that at the academy?"

"They taught us that," she responded as politely as she could, then obviously surprised him by adding, "but they didn't say anything about having the ability to read minds."

His tone was dangerous. "I don't like flippant remarks, McIntyre."

She was in a no-win situation and she knew it. "It wasn't meant to be flippant, sir. I'm just stating my side."

"I'm not asking you to be a mind reader," Barker told her tersely. "It's called second-guessing and playing hunches," he informed her. "If you want to survive here, you're going to have to learn how to do that." His tone was close to belligerent as he asked, "Think you can manage that, McIntyre?"

God, but she wanted to defend herself, to make this man back off and put him in his place. But she knew she couldn't. So she did her best to sound subdued, as if his sarcasm didn't affect her.

"Yes, sir."

"Good," he bit off. "Then we'll get along. Keep your partner alive, McIntyre, and he'll do the same for you."

With that, the lieutenant went back to his work.

She sat, listening to the sound of keys being struck, for another three minutes. He behaved as if she wasn't even in the office. Was this some kind of an endurance test? Or a contest of wills? How much longer was she expected to sit here?

Finally, she couldn't take it any longer. "Will there be anything else, sir?"

Barker kept on typing, the sound of his keys echoing rhythmically. "If there is, McIntyre, you'll know it," he told her, never looking up.

Was he dismissing her? She realized that she was gripping the armrests. That was twice today. So far, this was not shaping up to be one of her better days. She bit back her temper.

"Then I can go?"

Two more keys were struck before Barker gave her an answer. "Please."

Riley left the office without another word.

This couldn't possibly be what her stepfather had had in mind for her, she thought, shutting the lieutenant's door behind her. It took maximum control not to slam it in her wake. She knew that Brian Cavanaugh liked his lieutenants to be in charge and authoritative, but Barker came across like a petulant dictator.

This was not going to go well, she reflected.

She supposed she could go to her stepfather and tell him what had just transpired, how Barker had all but ignored her and definitely treated her with a lack of respect. But that would be tantamount to whining and she absolutely refused to come across like some spoiled brat.

She'd always pulled her own weight. She was proud of that. Riley saw no reason to change now.

Somehow, she promised herself, she was going to get through this and show that pompous jerk of a lieutenant that she wasn't about to retreat like some overly indulged, know-nothing rookie.

Looking around the squad room, she spotted Wyatt sitting at a desk. More accurately, her new temporary partner was leaning back in his chair, rocking it in such a precarious manner that the chair appeared in danger of tilting backward and crashing to the floor.

Great, Wyatt still hadn't grown up yet.

Better and better.

Releasing a sigh, Riley quickly crossed over to her partner. The sooner she got to work, the sooner she could figure out her role here.

Nodding at her, Sam righted his chair. "How did it go?" he asked cheerfully.

"It didn't," she ground out.

Wyatt didn't bother trying to suppress the knowing grin that came to his lips. "A little conflict of personalities, perhaps?"

The man shot from being a possible ally to an antagonist in the space of a split second. "You think it's funny?" she demanded hotly.

Riley noticed that several of the people in the room were looking in their direction. She would have to work on lowering her voice.

"Yeah, I do," he replied. Before she could fashion a comeback, he added, "That gives us something in common. Actually," he went on, glancing around the area, "that gives you something in common with every man in this squad room."

Every man.

Until he'd slapped a singular gender to the occupants of the room, Riley hadn't consciously realized that she was the only female on the floor. Since each desk wasn't occupied, she just assumed that some of them belonged to women who were out in the field. Female detectives were a common occurrence where she came from. Her mother had been out in the field prior to being wounded. Her sister, Taylor, and the female Cavanaugh cousins who had come as part of the package deal when her mother married the chief, were all currently working in the field.

In fact, as far as she knew, there were only two Cavanaugh women, Patience and Janelle, who weren't part of the police department and even they were closely associated with it. Patience was a vet who took care of the K-9 squad and was married to a police officer and Janelle was an assistant district attorney. She too was married to a police detective.

Being the only woman in the room felt rather unusual to her.

After scanning the area, she looked at Sam again. "There're no women on the floor?"

"On the floor?" he echoed. "Yes. In the department?" which was what he figured she actually meant, "No. As fate would have it, you'd be robbery division's first female detective." He flashed her a grin, clearly amused by the situation. "Think you're up to it, McIntyre?"

He was saying that to goad her, she thought. To make her stop focusing on the uncomfortable aspect of this situation and just view it as a challenge. Appreciating the intent, she had to give him his due. "You're not as dumb as you look, Wyatt."

The comment made him laugh. "Bet you say that to all the guys."

"Only the ones who deserve it." She wanted to settle in, even if it was just for the time being. "Okay, where do I sit?"

His eyes met hers. "Any place you plant your butt,

McIntyre. I'd say 'pretty butt,' but then you'd probably have me hauled up to human resources on harassment charges."

Okay, he obviously needed to know some basic ground rules about her.

"I don't need anyone to fight my battles for me, Wyatt. If something you say bothers me—more than normal," she qualified, "I'll let you know. I won't resort to running off to a go-between."

She wasn't sure, but she thought she saw respect enter his eyes.

"Fair enough," Wyatt declared with a nod of his head before flashing that now famous grin. "You know, McIntyre, this might be the beginning of a beautiful friendship."

"Too late for that. I already know you," she reminded him.

The look in his eyes told her that she was a long way off from that.

"There's knowing a person to nod at and say hello to, and then there's working with him. That, Detective McIntyre, is a whole different ball game," Wyatt assured her.

He was right, she thought grudgingly. Right because it involved exactly what that pompous ass in the glass office had referred to just before she had left his office. She would have Wyatt's life in her hands and Wyatt would have hers. That made for a bond that wasn't usually formed between two average acquaintances.

"Her," Riley finally corrected him. "Working with *her*."

His next words surprised her. Mainly because she was aware of his reputation as a ladies' man.

"I'd rather not think of you as a girl, McIntyre. Or a woman," he added, anticipating that she was going to correct his age-related reference to her gender.

Her eyebrows drew together as she tried to fathom why Wyatt had said that. Moreover, how could he help but think of her in those terms? She *was* a woman. Or was this just a set up for some elaborate wisecrack on his part?

But she bit anyway. "What do you want to think of me as?"

"A slightly curvy guy will do." He spread his hands in a wide shrug. "If this is going to work between us, that's what you're going to have to be, McIntyre. A feminine-looking guy."

She sighed. "You're crazy, you know that, Wyatt?"

And, right now, she didn't exactly have high hopes that *any* of this was going to work. But this was what the chief wanted and she was not about to be the one rushing back to him, complaining. She refused to let a man she respected so highly think of her in an unflattering light.

About to remind Wyatt that he hadn't answered her as to where she was to sit, Riley decided to reword the question. "Where's my desk, Wyatt?"

He gestured to the one that was facing his. It looked just as cluttered as his own. As a matter of fact, on closer examination, it looked as if the folders on the desk had overflowed from his. She glanced at a couple of the ones on top.

"Whose files are these?" she asked Wyatt. The writing on top of the first folder looked vaguely like the writing on the notepad on Wyatt's desk.

"Mine," he told her, moving several of the folders back to his desk. "I kind of spread out after Evans left." He shrugged as he collected the rest and placed them on his desk. "You know how that is."

"No," she contradicted, "I don't."

Even though Sanchez's desk had faced hers like Wyatt's faced his old partner's, she had taken great pains to keep her things from inching onto Sanchez's desk, which she'd called "No Man's Land." After he had been murdered, she'd cleaned out the desk for the man's mother, placing everything into a box and bringing it to the woman's house herself. She recalled that the visit had ended with both of them in tears.

"Well, it's normal around here," Wyatt told her, adding in a knowing tone, "Trust me."

Trust me.

That summed up everything in two neat little words. In order for things to work—for *anything* to work— there had to be a certain amount of trust. But trust was exactly what was missing from her soul. She honestly didn't know if she could ever trust anyone outside the family again. Ever allow anyone to trust her again. Both ways, it was just too big a risk to take.

Chapter 3

It was officially Riley's first full day as part of the robbery division and her new partner was conspicuously absent from his desk.

At first, she thought he had just beaten her in and was engrossed in some task. She'd even envisioned him complaining to a sympathetic ear about this new partner who had been forced on him by the Chief of Ds.

But when the first hour dragged into the next with still no sign of Wyatt anywhere on the floor, Riley began to reexamine the situation.

Wyatt's computer wasn't on.

It had been on all day yesterday, even when they went to interview a pawnbroker on the other side of Aurora whose shop had been burglarized. Like everyone else, Wyatt turned his computer on in the morning and then left it that way all day. He'd even doubled back last night to turn off the machine before he left the squad room for the evening.

Was his being out some reflection on her? Maybe his silent way of protesting being forced to pair up with her?

Riley frowned. She had no answers and a ton of questions that began to multiply.

"McIntyre!"

Her head snapped up the second the lieutenant had barked out her name. The man stood in the doorway of his office, glaring her way. Riley was on her feet instantly, ready to be sent on police business or hurry to his office, whatever the martinet of a commanding officer dictated.

"Yes, sir?"

Barker appeared mildly pleased that she had whipped into shape so quickly. The next second the look was gone. A deep frown had taken over his craggy, hard-as-nails features as he asked, "Where's your partner?"

How was she supposed to know? she asked silently. She wasn't Wyatt's mother or his keeper.

Out loud, Riley said, "I don't know, Lieutenant. Didn't he call in?"

Barker watched her as if she lacked the intelligence of a single-celled amoeba.

"If Wyatt'd called in, I'd know where he was, wouldn't I?" Sarcasm dripped from every word. "You're on a new case as of right now, McIntyre. Find your partner and tell him to drag himself in here. This isn't a country club."

If it was, she'd be handing in her membership card right about now, Riley thought. "No, sir."

About to turn back to his desk, the lieutenant stopped and leveled a dark look at her over his shoulder. Even across the room, it appeared lethal in nature.

"'No, sir?'" Barker echoed, his thin eyebrows narrowing into a vee.

Riley immediately realized what Barker was thinking—and her mistake. She lost no time in clarifying her response.

"No, sir, this isn't a country club. Yes, sir, I'll track down Detective Wyatt."

Barker nodded, momentarily appeased. "See that you do, McIntyre," he ordered. "God save us from loose cannons and mavericks," he muttered under his breath, retreating again into his glass-walled office.

Riley's survival instinct warred with her desire to be a good detective, no matter what department she was assigned to. Good detective won out.

She crossed the room and knocked on the lieutenant's door, even though it was still open. "Um, sir?"

"What are you still doing here, McIntyre?" he demanded without looking up, some obvious sixth sense identifying her for him. "I gave you an assignment."

"Yes, sir, but this is about the assignment after this one." She saw that she had him confused. "The new one for Wyatt and me."

"Home invasion," he snapped out, then rattled off an address. It was in the better part of the city and not all that far from her own, she noted. "Details are similar to the case Wyatt worked on last month. The first is still an open case. I want it closed."

It wasn't a suggestion, but a direct order.

The administrative assistant on their floor gave Riley her partner's address and phone number, along with an unsolicited comment.

Virginia McKee, the perpetually perky assistant, wrote down the information in a bold hand and offered the slip of paper to Riley.

"Enjoy," Virginia told her with a wink that was anything but subtle.

Riley folded the paper, but kept it in her hand rather than tuck it into her pocket. "There's nothing to enjoy. The lieutenant's looking for him."

"You're wrong there," Virginia contradicted, a sly smile curving her lips.

If she was going to survive here for a while, Riley knew she had to make allies and come across as friendly even though right now, being friendly was her last desire. This had to be her stepfather's goal when he had transferred her here. The business of living and acclimating to a new situation put things into some kind of perspective and forced her to move forward.

"Oh?"

Virginia indicated the paper she'd just given her. "There's a *lot* to enjoy there."

Spoken like a woman who's been there, Riley thought. Apparently, Sam Wyatt was still just as much of a player as he'd ever been. She knew he'd been when they were in the academy together. As she recalled, if it had a pulse, the required body parts and a smile, Wyatt considered it fair game.

It was to Wyatt's credit that he wasn't pushy about it, but then, a guy with Sam Wyatt's face and build didn't have to be. Most of the time, what he needed was the proverbial stick in order to beat back the hordes of women.

Not her concern one way or another, Riley told herself.

Armed with the number of Wyatt's landline, Riley didn't bother going back to her desk to make the call. Instead, she walked out into the hallway, stopped in an alcove next to the women's restroom and called her missing partner on her cell phone.

The phone on the other end of the line rang five times. The sixth ring had the answering machine picking up. Riley frowned.

Was Wyatt playing hooky? When the beep sounded, she started talking.

"Wyatt, this is McIntyre. The lieutenant wants to know where you are. He wanted me to tell you that you'd better haul your tail in if you know what's good for y—" She stopped abruptly as she heard the phone being picked up. "Wyatt?"

"Yeah, look, I'm not coming in today. Tell Barker I'm taking a sick day."

He sounded pretty agitated. Big night gone bad? she wondered. "How sick are you?"

"I've never felt like this before in my life," was his vague response.

Riley hesitated for a moment, not completely convinced that he wasn't pulling her leg. But then, what if he really was sick? As far as she knew, he lived alone. Maybe he needed someone to pick up medication for him. As his partner, it fell to her.

"Flu?"

"No," he bit off.

It was the middle of October and the Santa Ana winds were kicking up, making half the population of California miserable by playing havoc with their allergies and sinuses. The partner she'd had before Sanchez was wedded to his box of tissues the entire time the winds blew. Maybe Wyatt had the same problem.

"Sinus infection?" she guessed.

"No."

This time, he sounded downright surly. Her patience was slipping away. "Then what've you got?"

There was a long pause on the other end of the line. She was about to ask if he was still there when she heard him say, "I've got a kid."

"You've got what?"

"A kid," he repeated, doing his best not to shout. "Look, I'll be in tomorrow."

The line went dead against her ear before she could press him any further.

Sam let the receiver fall into its cradle and looked at the perfect little bit of humanity sitting on his sofa, politely pretending to be absorbed in the educational programming he'd turned on for her.

Six years old, she seemed to have already mastered

everything the multicolored, furry, perky little creatures prancing across the screen could possibly teach her.

From the moment he'd hit puberty and discovered it exceedingly to his liking, Sam had never felt at a loss as to what to do in *any* given situation.

Except now.

What the hell was he going to do with her?

Nothing he'd gone through these last twenty years had prepared him for this. But "this" had definitely happened. And now it was up to him to deal with it responsibly.

Oh, damn.

Sam scrubbed his hand over his face, forcing himself to think. But rather than coming up with a game plan, all he could do was relive the morning's earthshaking events in his mind. It sounded like a dramatic assessment to anyone privy to what had transpired, but as far as he was concerned, it *was* dramatic.

He'd never been a father before.

He'd always thought that eventually he'd like to be one. But he'd just assumed that the timing would be of his own choosing and only after he'd married someone he felt completed his world. Currently, no candidates qualified for that position. But he'd obviously joined fatherhood without first acquiring the required wife.

What was he going to do?

When the doorbell rang this morning just as he'd finished getting ready for work, the thought that it was his new partner had flashed through his brain. Not that he was expecting her—or anyone—but if it was going to be someone, for some unknown reason, his money was on McIntyre.

He would have lost. Big time.

When he opened the door, there standing in his doorway was a woman he'd never seen before. She held the hand of an almost doll-like, perfect little girl. Petite, blond, blue-eyed, the girl already had the makings of a little princess. It vaguely registered that the little girl didn't look a thing like the dark-haired woman whose hand she was holding.

"I'm afraid you've got the wrong apartment," he'd said to the woman.

The woman appeared unwilling to leave. "Detective Wyatt?"

His "Yes?" had been wary. Life on the force had made him privy to the world's darker elements.

"Sam Wyatt?" the woman pressed.

"Yes." His eyes had narrowed as he'd studied the woman in his doorway. "Do I know you?" It was a gratuitous question because he prided himself on never forgetting a face.

"No. But you 'knew' Lisa's mother." She nodded toward the little girl. "In the biblical sense," she emphasized. "Andrea Coltrane."

He never forgot a name, either. When the woman mentioned Andrea, an image instantly materialized in his mind's eye. It was accompanied by half a dozen memories that spliced together in a quick mental slideshow.

Andrea, a cool, statuesque blonde, proved to be a red-hot lover. So hot that for a very short while, he'd contemplated entering into a long-term relationship with the upwardly mobile tax attorney, but he never got the chance.

Inexplicably, things suddenly cooled between them. Before he knew it, Andrea had disappeared from his life. He'd tried calling her a couple of times. The second time, he'd been informed by a metallic voice that the number he'd dialed was no longer in service. When he discovered that she'd moved as well, he figured he would take the hint.

It never occurred to him that Andrea had moved for any other reason than she'd wanted a change. During their time together, she'd insisted that she wanted no strings tying her down.

Glancing at the little girl, an uneasy feeling told him that he'd made the wrong assumption.

"Where is Andrea?" he asked the woman, his tone guarded.

Rather than answer, the woman handed him an eight-by-ten manila envelope and then, still holding the little girl by the hand, she walked into his apartment.

"I'm Carole Gilbert. I worked with Andrea for the last five years." She nodded at the envelope. "This'll explain everything."

Worked.

Sam'd had an uneasy feeling that there was a specific reason for the reference in the past tense, probably not because Andrea had moved on again.

Fingers poised over the envelope's clasp, he'd raised his eyes to look at Carole. "What am I going to find in here?"

"In a nutshell, 'Congratulations, Detective Wyatt,

you've just become a daddy.' She moved the little girl forward. "This is your daughter, Lisa. She's six." Carole bent down so that her face was close to the little girl's. "Say hello to your father, Lisa," Carole instructed gently.

Cornflower blue eyes widening ever so slightly, the little girl gave him a shy smile and in a voice that was soft and delicate as the first spring breeze, she said, "Hello."

Everything inside of Sam shouted *no!* even as he found himself looking down into *Andrea's* blue eyes. Lisa was Andrea's daughter, all right. A perfect miniature of her mother.

The word "perfect" really was not applicable here, he'd thought as he felt his stomach sinking past his knees.

Despite the fact that she appeared anxious to leave, Sam made the bearer of his unsettling news stay as he read, then reread the letter and the will enclosed. And then he fired questions at her as he tried to reconcile himself to this wildly abrupt turn of events.

Andrea, killed the week before by a drunk driver, had left very specific instructions as to whom was to take care of Lisa in the event of her untimely death. An only child whose parents were both deceased, Andrea had felt that Lisa needed to be raised by at least one parent and he, Sam, met that minimum requirement.

He stared at the birth date that Andrea had written down. Apparently Lisa was the direct result of the "wildly romantic" two months he and Andrea had spent together. When she'd discovered that she was pregnant, Andrea was determined to raise Lisa on her own and so she had disappeared.

"'Nothing against you, Sam,'" he read. "'But at the time, you didn't strike me as exactly father material. But since you're reading this, circumstances have obviously dictated otherwise. Lisa is a wonderful, intelligent little girl—with us as her parents, how could she not be?— who needs your love and support now. I wish I could be there to see it. Take good care of her. She is the precious gift that keeps on giving.'"

He'd folded the letter knowing, for the first time, exactly what a butterfly pinned and mounted on a display board felt like.

After answering more questions and giving him the key to Andrea's apartment where the rest of Lisa's belongings and other important documents were stored, Carole left. Due to coercion on his part, she'd given him a number where she could be reached. A work number, but at least it was something.

He wasn't good at talking to females under the age of twenty-one but he knew that, barring an eleventh-hour miracle of some sort, he would have to learn. And learn fast.

Sam couldn't shake the feeling that he was the child and she the adult. When he spoke to her, Lisa seemed to gently humor him, going along with his suggestion for breakfast—only eggs since he didn't think that a six-year-old drank coffee—and settling on the sofa to watch television when he turned on the set for her.

When Sam heard the doorbell ring again less than an hour after Carole's departure, hope suddenly sprang up in his chest. He thought—fervently prayed—that Carole had suddenly changed her mind about turning over the little girl to him and had, instead, decided that it would be best for all to take her in.

He lost no time hurrying to open the door.

Hope died a cruel, quick death, crashing to the ground like a falling comet.

"Oh, it's you." As an afterthought, he stepped to the side to allow Riley to enter.

But Riley remained where she was. He looked really shaken up, light years away from the smooth operator she had been with yesterday.

"You can cancel the marching brass band, Wyatt. Fanfare would only embarrass me," Riley quipped, then got down to why she was here. "Lieutenant Barker's fit to be tied."

His lieutenant's disposition was extremely low on Sam's list of concerns at the moment. But he needed to work, now more than ever. This little accident of nature would need to be fed and clothed. And sent off to college. If he was lucky, she'd turn out to be a genius, going through grades at an accelerated rate and displaying the kind of intellectual acumen that attracted scholarships.

He eyed Riley warily. So far his luck had been running rather poorly this morning. "What did you tell him?"

"That you were following up on a lead and I was meeting you at the possible suspect's house. He wants us to hand off that case to Rafferty and Kellogg," she said, mentioning two other robbery detectives. "Seems that another home invasion went down last night. They only got the 9-1-1 call an hour ago. Details of the invasion are similar to one that you were already handling. Then Barker grumbled something about loose cannons and mavericks and retreated into his lair. My guess is that he's been watching too many action movies."

Finished, she peered around her partner's arm into the apartment. Since Wyatt hadn't actually voiced an invitation, she decided to take matters into her own hands and crossed the threshold.

"What was all this about you coming down with a case of 'kid'?" she asked. "Is that short for something?"

"Yeah." Sam closed the door behind her and gestured for Riley to follow him to the living room. "It's short for 'big trouble.'"

About to ask him what he was babbling about, the next minute, she caught sight of the little blond girl on the sofa and had her answer.

Chapter 4

Standing just a few feet inside the apartment, Riley looked from the child seated on the sofa to Wyatt and then back again. Surprise mingled with disbelief. The little girl, who had a box and a couple of suitcases beside her, was the very last thing she'd expected to find in Wyatt's apartment.

She flashed a wide smile at the little girl. As an official Cavanaugh by marriage, Riley was now an aunt, by proxy, to a whole slew of children coming in all sizes, shapes and ages. Children represented innocence, a clean slate.

Everyone should remain a child for as long as possible, she thought, a wave of protectiveness washing over her.

Crossing into the living room, Riley was aware that Wyatt was behind her. "Hi," she said to the little girl. "I'm Riley. What's your name?"

"Lisa," came the prompt, polite response.

Riley looked back at Wyatt for some kind of enlightenment. "Your niece?" she guessed.

Rather than answer, Sam took her by the arm and led her to the kitchen.

But before he got there, Lisa raised her voice and called out after her, "I'm his daughter."

Riley froze just shy of the kitchen and looked up at her partner. "Did she just say...?"

There was no childlike lisp, no baby voice to misunderstand. Lisa's enunciation was perfect, the kind that belonged to precocious, budding geniuses poised to take the world by storm.

Sam nodded. "Yes."

Riley was sure she was still missing something. "She's your daughter," she said, leaving it as a statement.

This time the single world came out like an angry cannon shot. "Yes."

The police department had been growing in recent years, but they were still pretty much a tight community. There were fewer detectives than uniformed cops. Word got around. There was never even a hint that Wyatt was anything but an available stud. If a short person was in the wings, someone would have mentioned it in passing.

"Since when?" she said.

He glanced over her head toward the living room and the child with flawless posture. He used to curl up on the sofa when he watched TV at her age. With her hands folded in her lap and sitting ramrod straight, Lisa looked as if she was attending a meeting instead of watching television.

"Apparently since six years ago," he told Riley with a sigh.

Riley studied him for a moment. The detective seemed unsettled. They hadn't interacted very much in the last few years, but to her recollection, she'd never seen him rattled before.

"How long have you known?" she asked.

Sam looked at his watch. "Two hours, give or take a few minutes."

He wasn't volunteering anything, so she started piecing things together herself.

"This woman who obviously can keep a secret, she just left her daughter with you? Just like that?" Riley knew it happened but it was difficult to envision.

He had no idea why, but he suddenly felt defensive for Andrea. "She didn't have much choice, seeing as how she's—" His voice dropped before he said the last word. "—dead."

Thoroughly confused, Riley looked over her shoulder into the living room. "If her mother's dead, how did Lisa—"

Wyatt cut her off before she could finish. "Her friend brought Lisa over, along with a letter from Andrea and a copy of Andrea's will."

According to the document, his new daughter had a small trust fund set aside in her name. But she couldn't touch it until she turned eighteen. Twelve years from now, he thought.

The name meant nothing to Riley. "I take it Andrea was your—" She left the sentence unfinished, searching for the right word, hoping that Wyatt would supply it.

"Andrea wasn't anything of mine," he denied vehemently.

As far as he was concerned, until this morning, Andrea belonged to his past. Just one of the women he'd dated. Except now she wasn't. She was the mother of his child. The child that, less than three hours ago, he didn't even know he had.

"Well, she must have been 'something' of yours if that little girl in the next room really is your daughter." All sorts of thoughts rushed through her mind. She asked the first logical one that occurred to her. "Are you sure that she's yours?"

"If you mean did she come with DNA test results, then no. But there was no reason for Andrea to lie." Especially since the woman had never come to him with this news while she was alive and able to forge her own path. "Andrea is—was—a very independent woman." Even though she hadn't been part of his life for over six years, it was hard to think of the woman in the past tense. "This also explains a lot of things," he said more to himself than to Riley.

"Such as?" Riley coaxed, her curiosity jacked up to high.

For a second, he'd almost forgotten his partner was here.

"Why she disappeared so abruptly," he said. "One day she was there and we were talking about clearing out a drawer for her and giving her some space in my closet. The next," he snapped his fingers, "she was gone."

"Despite the enticing offer of a drawer and four hangers?" Riley marveled. "Woman didn't know when she had it good, huh?"

He looked at her, annoyed. "Sarcasm doesn't suit you."

"Funny, I always thought it did." Riley grew serious and asked, "Did you even try to find her after she disappeared?"

Ordinarily, he might not have. But then, no other woman had just vanished the way Andrea had. "Yes, I tried to find her."

"Obviously not hard enough." She saw that he took offense, so she told him why she felt that way. "You're a detective, Wyatt. Finding things—like people—is what you do. And yet, in this case, you didn't."

He blew out a frustrated breath. Maybe Riley was right. Maybe, deep down, he didn't want to find Andrea if she had thought so little of him to leave without a word. He wished now that he had pushed harder.

"Yeah, well, she moved, changed jobs, changed her phone number. For all I knew, she changed her name." He shrugged, trying to dismiss the incident. "I figured she got spooked."

This man couldn't have spooked a woman, she thought, dismissing his excuse. He was the kind of man that drew women.

"That's what you get for wearing your Godzilla suit when it's not even Halloween," she cracked.

"Spooked by the idea of commitment," he elaborated. He saw her opening her mouth, ready to argue the point. "You know, it's not just guys who have trouble wrapping their heads around making a commitment. Women have trouble with the concept, too."

Riley relented. She really couldn't argue with that. Her own sister, Taylor, was part of that group—until love ambushed her and tossed a tall, dark, handsome private investigator in her path. Now, she knew, Taylor couldn't begin to imagine life without J.C.

But rather than share this with Wyatt, she merely asked, "So you let her go?"

"I decided not to come on like a stalker," he corrected. "It was good while it lasted, but I assumed when she took off like that, whatever we had was over."

Riley glanced back at the little girl in the living room. Lisa was still sitting ramrod straight, watching television.

"Apparently not," Riley pointed out, then asked. "What's your next move?"

That was the sixty-four-million-dollar question. "Hell if I know."

Riley held up one finger. "Okay, first move. No more cursing."

"I wasn't cursing," Sam protested.

"Not by the standards we're used to," she allowed, "but 'hell' and 'damn' are curses of the venial variety." He looked unconvinced, so she explained further. "Think of it in the same terms as marijuana leading the user to cocaine. Both are illegal drugs, one just viewed as far more serious than the other. Next," she continued, now holding up a second finger, "you need to line up someone to stay with Lisa while you're working."

He hadn't even thought that far ahead yet. It was as if his brain was paralyzed, still trying to deal with this major curve. Now that he did think about it, it didn't help. There was no one to turn to.

"Everyone I know is at the precinct."

He'd never mentioned any relatives when they had attended the academy. Riley realized that she had no idea what his family dynamics were like. "No family to fall back on?"

He had family, or rather, a parent. His father, who lived in a retirement community. "In Arizona. Kind of a killer commute."

Riley stopped listening when he mentioned Arizona. "Let me see what I can do," she said, taking out her cell phone.

When she pressed a button on the keypad, he asked, "Who are you calling?"

Riley held up her hand, silently asking him to hold his thought until she got off the phone.

"Brenda? Hi, it's Riley. Look, I know that this is really short notice and I hate to impose on you, but my partner needs someone to watch his little girl—Six," she said in response to the question her stepbrother's wife asked her. "Her mother's dead and—" Again Riley paused, this time not for a question but to listen while Brenda expressed her sympathy for both her partner and his daughter. The next sentence had her smiling broadly. "Thanks, Brenda, you're a doll. We'll be over as soon as we can." With that, she slipped the cell phone closed again.

"Over where?" Wyatt pressed the second she ended the call.

"Brenda is one of the chief's daughters-in-law. She's married to Dax and she just said to bring Lisa over. Brenda works out of her house a lot so she can raise her own kids," Riley explained, then added, in case Wyatt needed further convincing, "She used to be a teacher. And she's great with kids. This way, you can appease the lieutenant and get back to work, and you get a little breathing space to calmly figure out how to proceed."

"Calmly," Sam echoed, shaking his head. His mouth curved in a smile he definitely didn't feel. "Too late. The ship has sailed on that one."

It might be better if he just took the day off after all. She took out her phone again. "Want me to call Brenda back and say you've changed your mind about bringing Lisa over?"

No, Riley was right. He should get back to work and he needed time to think. "What I really want is for you to turn the clock back six years and make sure you kick me in the pants when I suggest going to Malone's for a drink." Malone's was the bar where he had first met Andrea. She had been there with her friends, celebrating a major court-room win. She'd gone home with him that night.

Riley filled in the blanks herself, surmising that he had to be referring to approximately the time when Lisa had been conceived.

"Much as that's a very tempting offer, Wyatt, I first have

to point out that you mean seven years ago, not six. Nine months after conception, remember?" she prodded. "And second, magic and/or time travel are not part of my job description or, by any stretch of the imagination, my résumé."

Riley waited for her partner's response, but there was none. His eyes almost glazed over. She suspected that fatherhood bursting upon him like an exploding land mine was to blame.

She waved her hand in front of his eyes. "Earth to Wyatt, earth to Wyatt."

Catching her by the wrist, Sam pushed her hand back down. "What?"

"Do you or don't you want to take your daughter to Brenda's house?" she asked.

Sam supposed that solved the problem today but what about tomorrow? And all the tomorrows to come, what of them? He couldn't think about that now. They'd just have to work themselves out somehow. He had to believe that.

She was still watching him, waiting. "That would be good," he finally told her.

She crossed back into the living room. "Lisa, honey, your father and I are going to take you to this nice lady's house. Her name's Brenda. Brenda Cavanaugh."

Lisa slowly slid off the sofa, never taking her eyes from the man Carole had told her was her father. "To stay?" she asked hesitantly. "Don't you want me?"

Riley thought she saw the little girl's lower lip tremble as she asked the last question. Her heart twisted a little in sympathy.

"Of course he wants you," Riley said before Wyatt

had a chance to answer. "But he works, honey. As a police detective."

She turned toward Wyatt. "Isn't that right, Detective Wyatt?" she asked, keeping her voice purposely sweet.

He merely nodded, not unlike a man about to slip into shock.

"Wyatt, you okay?" she asked.

Sam waved off her concern. "I'll get the car started."

To her knowledge, his car didn't need to be warmed up but she didn't contradict him. Instead, she turned her attention to the little girl. She did her best to sound cheerful and reassuring. "Need help packing something to take with you?"

Lisa eyed her uncertainly. "Then I am staying at this other person's house?"

Lisa's voice was soft and low, but it seemed to Riley to hum with intelligence.

"Just for a few hours. You'll be coming back here later today. Tonight at the latest," Riley augmented. As detectives, they did have shifts, but their hours could still be rather erratic. If that home invasion had been reported last night, she had no doubt that both Wyatt and she would have gotten calls in the middle of the night to come to the scene of the crime.

She saw the solemn look on Lisa's face. Tears began to fill the little girl's eyes. Was she afraid? "What's the matter?"

Lisa swallowed before answering. "That's what Mama said before she left me. She didn't come back."

Riley bent down to embrace Lisa. She felt the little

girl stiffen at first, then melt into her arms. Poor thing just wants to be loved, she thought.

"Honey, your mama was in a car accident." As she spoke, Riley stroked Lisa's hair soothingly. "She wanted nothing more than to come back to you, but well, it didn't turn out that way."

Lisa raised her head to look up at her. "You'll come back?"

Riley rose to her feet. "We'll come back," she promised. She crossed her heart before she took the little girl's hand in hers.

Lisa asked her the same question again just before she and Wyatt left.

Wyatt was ahead of her, obviously anxious to get going. He said a quick goodbye to Lisa. She looked so lost, standing there so forlornly, that Riley bent down and hugged her. That was when Lisa asked her again. "You'll come back?"

"Your dad'll come back, honey," she promised, thinking that Lisa meant her question for Wyatt. "I guarantee it."

"No, you," Lisa corrected urgently. "You'll come back?"

Riley exchanged looks with Wyatt, caught off guard by Lisa's question. This wasn't the time for a philosophical debate as to her place in the scheme of things—or rather her lack of a place.

Instead, she rose to her feet and promised, "I'll come back. We both will."

Only then did Lisa's anxious expression begin to relax. "Okay."

Brenda moved forward, slipping her arm around the girl's shoulders. "C'mon, Lisa, let me introduce you to my kids."

Lisa allowed herself to be led away, although she kept looking over her shoulder at them until Wyatt closed the front door, effectively separating them from his daughter's view.

He blew out a breath as if he'd been holding it the entire time they'd been at Brenda's house. "Looks like she's already bonded with you."

Was that relief she saw in his eyes? "If her mother never married, Lisa's probably more comfortable around women."

"Great," he murmured under his breath.

"You'll rise to the challenge," she assured him. "Granted Lisa's a bit younger than you're used to, but once you turn on that charm, I'm sure you'll have her eating out of your hand." Her attempt to tease him out of his solemnity failed. She dropped her kidding tone. "What's the matter?"

He paused by his car. "I don't think I can be a father, McIntyre," he told her.

"You're perfectly normal. I'd say probably ninety-five percent of all fathers say that at the beginning."

"Yeah, but they all get nine months to get used to the idea. I didn't even get nine seconds. One minute I'm a bachelor. The next, I'm a family man," he complained, shaking his head.

Riley gave him a knowing look. "As I remember it, you were always a quick study. You'll get the hang of this in no time."

For the first time since she'd sat in front of him at the academy, Wyatt didn't look his usual confident self. Instead, he appeared worried.

As he opened the door to his vehicle, he paused. "I've never said this before," he started to confess, then stopped.

"Go ahead," she coaxed.

It took him a couple more seconds to frame his admission. "I've never said this before," he began again. "But I'm going to need help." And then, after taking a breath, he came to the crux of his request. "In short, McIntyre, I'm going to need you."

Chapter 5

For just a split second, when Sam said he needed her, a whole different meaning to his words flashed through her mind. A meaning that had nothing to do with the present set of circumstances her partner was facing.

Riley pushed that, and the unsettling, restless curiosity away. "Need me to what?" she heard herself asking.

"Help me with Lisa."

What else could he have meant, idiot? she silently demanded. Out loud Riley tried to sound casual as she said, "I thought I was already helping. I'm the one who got you a babysitter for the day." And, if necessary, a more long-term arrangement could be made with Brenda for Lisa's after-school care.

School.

Sam said his daughter was six. That meant she belonged in school. Another onslaught of questions rushed at her, temporarily squeezing out the feeling she'd just experienced.

Sam nodded. For a moment, he forgot about getting into his car and driving to the scene of the home invasion. He needed to air this out, get it said and at least temporarily straight in his mind. "And I appreciate it in case I forgot to mention it—"

"You did."

He suppressed an impatient sigh, knowing he didn't want to do or say anything that would alienate this woman right now. He *did* need her. Besides, she was his partner.

"But this isn't some two-hour movie where everything gets neatly wrapped up and uplifting music plays as the credits begin to roll. This is real life, McIntyre." He didn't add that it was *his* life and he had no idea how he'd found himself in this predicament. He'd always been so careful. But nothing—including birth control obviously—was foolproof. "And there's an ocean of tomorrows to face."

It occurred to her that there might be a very simple solution to his problem, at least for the time being. "Well, 'Daddy,' don't you have a current girlfriend you can turn to?" Someone eager to cull his favor by pitching in to care for his daughter would be really handy right about now.

But Sam shook his head. "Not at the moment. I seem to be in between shallow relationships."

Her mouth curved. "Glad you said it and not me."

The way he saw it, it had been a preemptive strike. "Figured you would." He looked at her hopefully. "How about it, McIntyre?" he pressed. "Can you run interference for me?"

She knew he wanted her to take over. Maybe volunteer to take his daughter to her extended family and have one or more of them become responsible for Lisa.

Ain't gonna happen, Wyatt, she thought.

"No, but I can show up temporarily in the evening and lend you a hand if you like. You're going to have to be there, too," she specified. "In order to get used to each other, you and Lisa will have to actually *be* with each other."

Sam sighed and dragged a hand through his hair. The incredibly dry air sucked the moisture out of everything. He could feel static electricity crackling just above his scalp.

McIntyre was making sense, he knew that. But for the first time in his life, he felt unequal to the challenge that faced him. What did he know about raising a little girl? Or even interacting with one? He hadn't a clue.

But McIntyre did. He watched her as would a desperate man searching for a lifeline. "You've got a big family, right, McIntyre?"

"I do now," she qualified. Before the wedding, there had only been her brothers and her sister. Now, of course, besides the huge entourage she'd gained, there were also her siblings' better-halves to take into account. The size of her family had grown astronomically in a very short time. "Why? Are you thinking of trying to sneak Lisa in, hoping everyone just thinks she's part of the under-five-foot group?"

"Not exactly, but close," he admitted.

Riley shook her head. "Desperate doesn't look good on you," she told him, then smiled. "Don't worry, it'll be all right." A note of kindness entered her voice as she added, "And you'll have backup."

He would have preferred just handing off Lisa. Not because he was indifferent, or because having Lisa around would cramp his style—cute kids were known to attract women, not repel them—but because he didn't think it was fair to the little girl. She deserved to be raised by someone who knew what he was doing, not a father who would be stumbling around in the dark.

"Right," he muttered. He told himself to focus on work. "Okay, let's just table this for now. We need to get to this house before Barker has us shot." He opened the door on the driver's side.

After getting in, Riley found herself coaxing a reluctant seat belt to extend. On the way to Brenda's, she'd sat in the back with Lisa to make the girl not feel any more isolated than she probably already did. Riding shotgun in this case had its disadvantage.

"Want to sit in the back?" he proposed as he started the car.

"No," she bit off. She wasn't about to be defeated by a safety device.

It took her two hard tugs to properly extend the belt to the length where she could secure it around herself.

Holding onto it tightly, she slipped the metal tongue into its slot. That out of the way, Riley glanced at Wyatt.

He really did have one heck of a profile. No wonder he had to all but beat women off with a stick. The man was just too good-looking for his own good.

Or hers.

The thought surprised her. Riley searched for a safe topic, something to redirect her mind onto more neutral territory. She decided to ask about her new boss even though she could have just as easily asked one of her siblings, or her mother.

"How long has Barker been in charge of the department?"

Sam made a sharp right at the next light. The freeway he needed was just a block away. "For as long as I've been there."

That meant at least for the last five years. "Tell me, has he always had the personality of a piranha, or is that something new?"

Sam laughed, then felt duty bound to defend the man, at least a little. "Oh, he's a decent enough person—on his good days."

Neither yesterday nor today came under that heading. "These good days, do they happen with any kind of reliable frequency?" she asked. "Or are they like *Brigadoon*? Making an appearance once every hundred years?"

The reference she'd made meant nothing to him. He had no idea what or who Brigadoon was, but he let it go. "His wife left him a couple of years ago. It really tore him up."

"And he's been taking it out on everyone ever since?" she guessed.

Just making the light, Sam guided his vehicle onto the freeway. With rush hour over, traffic was flying this time of the morning.

"Something like that." He needed to focus on something other than his present situation. Maybe if he didn't think about it, a solution would eventually occur to him. "Did the lieutenant give you any details about this new case?"

Before leaving to find him, she'd gone back to her new superior to ask for any more information. The man had seemed annoyed and then tolerant. He'd spared her a few crumbs. She was glad now she'd asked. Though they knew each other, she and Wyatt had never worked a case together. She didn't want him thinking that he'd been harnessed with an idiot, there only because of her connections.

"Barker said the MO was like the home invasion you were already working on. No sign of a break-in, family bound in duct tape and held prisoner while two men dressed in black, wearing ski masks, systematically robbed the place. And when they were finished, they chloroformed the people so that they would be long gone before either of the victims could get loose and call the police."

Accelerating to pass a truck and take the off-ramp, Sam nodded. "Does sound like the other home invasion," he observed.

The bit about the chloroform had been left out of the

description they had released to the public. That was inside information only the victims and the thieves knew about.

"How far along are you on that case?" she asked.

He'd reached a dead end, which was why the lieutenant had assigned him to the case he'd just taken back today. "Would you like that in inches or centimeters?"

"That far, huh?"

Frustrated, he said, "Yeah, but now that you're here, we'll just whip right through the case and find the bad guys."

She silently counted to ten then said in a calm, neutral voice, "I don't think that sarcasm is the best way to go if you want my help."

Taking the off-ramp, Wyatt followed the winding path and found himself stuck at a red light. "You won't help me work the home invasion cases if your feelings are hurt?"

"I was talking about you needing my help with Lisa after we're off the clock."

He'd actually forgotten this newest development in his life for a second.

"Oh, right." He blew out a breath. "McIntyre, if I can't remember from one minute to the next that I'm supposed to be a father, how am I going to be one 24/7?"

She put herself in his place. This must have knocked him for a loop.

"First of all, you're new at it. Give yourself time to get used to the situation. Second, you're not 'supposed to be' a father. You *are* a father whether you like it or not. Your little 'play' time created a human being. Since you were the guy involved, that makes you the father.

The sooner you get used to it, Wyatt, the faster things'll start falling into place for you."

"What if I don't?" he asked.

He'd lost her. "Don't what?"

"Don't get used to it?" He paused for a second, then said what was really on his mind. "What if I don't want to be the dad?"

She tried to shift her body toward him but the seat belt held her tightly in place. "Are you talking about walking away?"

"I can do that?" he asked. Then, before she could form an answer that didn't have a slew of less-than-flattering names attached to it, Wyatt shot down his own question with a resigned sigh. "I can't do that. It's not her fault that she's here."

"I'd take the word 'fault' out of the conversation if I were you," she strongly advised. "Using it might undermine Lisa's worth in her own eyes if she happens to overhear you. As a matter of fact, I wouldn't go there at all."

"There?" he echoed, puzzled.

"The past," she explained. "How Lisa came to be, all that stuff. Get a paternity test if you want to. Then, if she turns out to be yours, accept the fact and go from there."

He didn't need a paternity test. As he'd told McIntyre earlier, there was no reason for Andrea to lie and the little girl's age gibed with when they were together. Lisa was his. He glanced at his partner. "You charge by the hour for this golden advice?"

He hid vulnerability behind sarcasm. She could identify with that. Her answer was as flippant as his question. "Since you're my partner, the first hundred hours are free."

Sam didn't completely suppress his groan as he contemplated hearing McIntyre's voice go on and on for the next one hundred hours. "I'd better start keeping track then."

The corners of her mouth curved. "I'll let you know when your time is up," she promised.

He felt like a man whose time was up already. But he couldn't think about that now, couldn't contemplate all the problems that lay ahead. He had a home invasion to investigate and—hopefully—solve.

Sam turned his vehicle onto the street where the invasion had taken place. "We're here," he announced.

"I never would have guessed," she cracked.

The breathtaking estate-sized house had a squad car parked in the middle of the driveway, forcing them to park at the curb. A crowd of curious people was being physically held back by several strategically positioned sawhorses. And even if none of that was there, the bright yellow crime scene tape across the front of the building would have been a dead giveaway.

Getting out of the car, Sam shook his head. "You'd think people living in this neighborhood would have a better security system in place."

She saw it differently. "On the contrary, people living here think they're safe *because* of the neighborhood. They plunk down money that once would have been

enough to buy them their own small European princi-
pality and they think that's enough to keep the bad guys
out, not realizing that the bad guys assume that the rich
are a bunch of wimps who won't offer any resistance if
confronted."

"I suppose that makes sense—in a perverse sort of
way," he allowed.

"Thank you." She took his comment as a compliment
and flashed him a smile before making her way toward
the front door. A stern-faced policeman stood before it
like a muscular roadblock. He made no attempt to move
out of her way. Riley held up her ID and her badge for
the officer to examine.

The stone face softened and took on mobility as the
officer looked from her wallet to her face.

"New on the job?" he asked, interest entering his
dark brown eyes.

"Just to the department," she corrected. "First full day."

"She's with me," Sam informed the beat policeman,
coming up behind her.

Recognition was immediate. "Oh, sorry, Detective
Wyatt. But you can't be too careful," he confided. "I
just had a reporter try to get inside by claiming he was
a relative."

"What gave him away?" Riley asked, curious.

A dimple appeared on his right cheek as he smiled.
"Got the victims' last name wrong," he told her, happy
to share the story.

"Keep up the good work," she said to the patrolman
as she followed Wyatt into the house.

Wyatt glanced at her over his shoulder. "What was that all about?"

"Just building goodwill," Riley told him. "I promised myself that if I ever made detective, I wouldn't forget where I came from and I wouldn't act cocky about my shield. We're all supposed to be on the same team, right?"

Was she for real? He thought he recalled her being more driven at the academy. "If you dip your finger into a cup of black coffee, does it become sickeningly sweet?"

She'd already made up her mind that he wasn't going to get under her skin no matter what he said. "I don't know. I'll have to try it someday. In the meantime, there's nothing wrong with wanting to get along with people."

"Didn't say that there was. I just like keeping the nausea level down." From the expression on her face, McIntyre wasn't listening to him anymore. Instead, her eyes were sweeping the area. The spiral staircase alone, leaving the entranceway on two sides rather than just the standard one, would have filled up over half his apartment. "What?" he prodded. This couldn't have been her first time in a house worth multiple millions.

She peered past the splendor, taking in, instead, the chaos. "This place looks like it was hit by a hurricane."

"It was. Two of them, actually," he said, referring to the fact that the victims had reported waking up to not one robber but two. "Thieves don't usually have to worry about being invited back. That frees them up to make as big a mess as they want while looking for things that make their risk-taking worthwhile."

She nodded, knowing that in this case, she was the

novice and he the experienced one. That meant she would have to follow his lead and, most likely, take orders from him—at least for the time being.

"How do you want to do this?" she asked.

He raised an eyebrow at the question. "Solving the case comes to mind."

"I mean, do you want to take the husband or the wife?"

Amused, knowing what she was after, he decided to yank her chain just a little. "They're being given away?"

"To question." She enunciated each syllable clearly, holding her exasperation in check.

"Why don't we make it a joint effort?" he suggested, his tone marginally patronizing. "That way, they won't feel as if they were being interrogated."

"I had no intentions of conducting an interrogation," she informed him. "I just thought we could compare stories after we finished, see if there're any inconsistencies. If we keep them together, they could keep each other in check."

He studied her for a long moment. What was going on in her head? he wondered. Despite his baiting her, he was aware that she was sharp. Had something occurred to her that he'd missed?

"You're assuming they have something to hide?" he asked.

"Not exactly, but maybe the wife wanted to get away from the husband and this so-called robbery could be a way of funding her escape. Or maybe she found out he was having an affair and she wanted to get even with him by scaring him. Then again, he might have wanted—

what?" she finally asked, unable to handle the way Wyatt looked at her any longer. She got the feeling that she provided him with his morning's entertainment.

"Homicide has certainly left its mark on you, hasn't it?"

"Being a good cop has left its mark on me," she informed him. "No stone unturned," she elaborated.

He rolled her suggestion over in his head. "Okay, have it your way. I'll take the husband, you take the wife—unless you'd rather have it the other way around. You get the guy and I take the woman."

"No, the first way's fine," she said. "Mrs. Wilson will probably feel better talking to a woman about what happened than someone who looks like he'd just finished a photo shoot for *GQ*."

"I could rub a little dirt on my sleeve if you think that'll make me look more capable."

"Now who's being sarcastic?" she asked.

He held up his hand. "That would be me. C'mon, we'll get this over with and let these people rest."

"You really think they can sleep after what happened?" she asked.

This morning's events had really shaken him up, Sam thought, annoyed with himself. He wasn't thinking clearly. "I guess not," he grudgingly admitted.

Directed by another officer on the scene, they walked into the living room where they found the couple, still in their nightclothes and frightened, like two people who had been through a nightmare. They sat on an expensive-looking, oversized yellow leather sofa, apparently unwilling or unable to move. Trapped in their own world, they seemed oblivious to all the crime scene investigators and police personnel moving about the area.

At least there was no need for a medical examiner, Riley thought with relief.

"Mr. and Mrs. Wilson?" Wyatt addressed the tense couple respectfully. Two sets of frightened brown eyes turned toward him. "I'm Detective Wyatt and this is my partner, Detective McIntyre. We'll be taking your statements."

"We already gave statements," Mr. Wilson protested, a mixture of weariness and indignation in his voice.

"We know," Riley told them sympathetically, moving in front of Wyatt. Her eyes were on the husband the entire time. It didn't take a psychiatrist to know he felt emasculated by what had happened. "You're tired and angry and you just want to forget the whole thing ever happened. But it would really be very helpful if you both went over the events again. Maybe this time you might remember something that hadn't occurred to you when you gave your statement earlier."

The couple exchanged glances as if that helped them to decide their next course of action. And then the husband inclined his head, still not a hundred percent sold yet. "Well, if you think it'll help—"

"We do," Riley was quick to assure him.

Robert Wilson blew out a long breath. "I guess we can go through it one more time," he said with resignation.

"We appreciate your cooperation," Wyatt told him, feeling as if his words were coming after the fact. This new partner of his, he thought, was a regular little ball of fire.

Chapter 6

At the last moment, because the woman looked so shaken, Riley decided not to separate the couple as initially planned. When Wyatt began to ask the husband to come with him, she laid a hand on her partner's arm and minutely shook her head.

Confused, Wyatt took his cue, wondering if changing her mind was a common thing with her.

Still scowling, whether at them or the situation was unclear, Robert Wilson began talking, telling them the way the robbery went down.

"They came in while we were asleep—"

Unable to contain her nervous energy, his wife broke into the narrative with her own reaction to the events. "I thought I heard a noise. When I opened my eyes, they were standing over us. On either side of the bed," she added breathlessly. She covered the lower part of her face with trembling hands. She gave the impression that she was trying to smother a scream. "It was awful."

"How many of them were there again?" Sam asked, looking at Mrs. Wilson now.

"Two." Shirley Wilson blurted out the word as if she couldn't keep it in her mouth a second longer.

"Two that we saw," her husband corrected, giving her a condescending look. Shirley Wilson's eyes widened with fear.

Sam's attention shifted back to Wilson. "Do you think there were more?"

Wilson appeared to lose all semblance of patience. "How should I know?" he snapped.

"No, there were only two," Shirley told them. "I'm sure of it."

"Right. The expert," Wilson grumbled darkly.

"What happened next?" Riley asked, trying to get the couple focused on the details of what had transpired during the robbery instead of arguing with each other.

It was obvious to her that Wilson and his wife were both scared in their own fashion. In addition, she was sure Robert Wilson felt more than a little humiliated because he couldn't protect either his home or his wife. That had to shake a man up, mess with his self-image.

"They dragged us out of bed, tied us up," Wilson recited through clenched teeth, obviously resenting having to go through this again. "Then they put duct tape across our mouths—"

Shirley grabbed onto Riley's wrist, pulling the detective's attention toward her. "I thought I was going to suffocate," the woman cried in a whimpering, shaky voice.

"But you didn't, did you?" her husband pointed out tersely, glaring at her. It wasn't clear if he resented her interruption, or the fact that she was bringing further attention to the fact that he'd been helpless to come to her aid.

"No." His wife stared down at the floor. Not, Riley thought, unlike a dog that had been beaten. Her own resentment immediately shot up. She was about to say something to the man when Wyatt spoke.

"Mr. Wilson, we realize that you've been through a lot, but so has your wife. There's no need to keep snapping at her," Sam told him. His voice was calm, but an underlying strength resonated in his words. "Now both of you take a deep breath and let's go on."

"Can I get you some water?" Riley asked the woman. Clasping her hands together in her lap, Shirley shook her head. Riley shifted her eyes toward the woman's husband. "You?" she asked more formally.

"I'd like a scotch," Wilson responded, frustrated. A huge sigh escaped his lips. "No, I'm okay," he amended.

"What happened next?" Sam coaxed.

Wilson seemed to brace himself. "They made us sit in chairs and tied us to them. Then they emptied our house."

"How long were they here?" Riley asked.

Wilson shrugged. There seemed to be no way to gauge time. "Maybe an hour at the most."

"It felt like forever," Shirley chimed in over his voice.

"And when they were finished, they put rags over our faces." Hysteria reentered her voice as she said, "I thought they were going to kill us—"

"They used chloroform," Wilson interrupted, talking over his wife. The disdain in his voice was impossible to miss. "Knocked us out so that we couldn't try to stop them."

"Like that could ever happen," Shirley murmured under her breath. It was still loud enough for all of them to hear.

Rising in his seat, Wilson looked as if he was about to argue with his wife again. Sam put his hand firmly on the man's shoulder, pressing him back down onto the sofa.

"You can tell it all to the marriage counselor later," Sam told him sternly. "Right now, we need a detailed list of everything that's missing."

"I don't know everything that's missing," Wilson snapped. "This is a big house, Officer—"

"Detective," Riley corrected before Sam had a chance to.

"Whatever," Wilson huffed out, dismissing the difference in title at the same time. "I just know they took most of my wife's jewelry." That brought up another bone of contention as he glared at her. "I *told* you to leave it in the safety deposit box at the bank."

"Then I'd have to go to the bank whenever I wanted to wear something," Shirley complained. By the sound of her voice, this wasn't a new argument. She turned to look at Riley, seeking an ally. "What's the point of having jewelry if you can't wear it?"

"Well, you certainly can't wear it now, can you?"

Wilson jeered. "Because *they've* got it," he emphasized heatedly.

This all had such a familiar ring to it, Riley thought, although her mother had never defended herself. For the sake of her children and hoping to cut the scene short, her mother had always let her father unload on her.

Riley hated the sound of an argument. "And the longer you bicker," she said, addressing them both, "the less of a chance we have of recovering anything."

"Who are you kidding?" Wilson demanded, turning on her. "You're both just going through the motions, covering your tails as it were. We're never going to see any of what those two made off with and you know it."

Sam answered before she could. "That's certainly true if you waste time arguing and don't cooperate," Sam told him coldly. Wilson shut his mouth. "Now is there anything else you remember?"

When Shirley looked at them blankly, Riley elaborated. "Did either of them have any kind of an accent? Or did either one of them slip up and call the other by a name?"

"They were just 'Smith' and 'Jones,'" Shirley told them.

"Those are aliases," Wilson shouted at her in disgust. Shirley looked at Riley, silently appealing to her to help.

Riley shook her head at Wilson. There was a smattering of sympathy in her expression. "Most likely," she agreed. "Can you remember anything else? Anything at all?"

Clearly frustrated as well as contrite, Shirley shook her head. Then suddenly, the light seemed to dawn in her eyes. "Wait a minute," she said excitedly. "Garlic." Looking from one to the other, she told them, "I remember garlic."

"Garlic?" Sam repeated uncertainly. He exchanged glances with his partner.

"What the hell are you babbling about now, woman?" Wilson demanded angrily.

This time Riley clamped her hand on the man's arm. "Mr. Wilson, don't have me ask you again to refrain from belittling your wife." She struggled to keep her voice level. "You've both been through an awful ordeal and you came out of it alive. That doesn't always happen with victims of a robbery," she emphasized. Turning toward the man's wife, Riley said, "Now, you were saying, Mrs. Wilson?"

"One of them smelled of garlic," she told Riley, then specified, "The one who tied me up. He seemed like the younger one."

"Because his ski mask wasn't as old as the other guy's?" Wilson asked, mocking his wife's assumption.

"Because his voice sounded younger," she answered him defiantly with a toss of her head.

Good for you, lady, Riley thought, keeping her expression deliberately blank.

"Anything else?" Sam coaxed, looking from one to the other. "Either of you?"

Not to be left out, Wilson repeated what had already been assessed. "They were thin, tall. And they seemed to know their way around."

That led them to one possibility. "Have you had any workmen in the house in the last six months?" Sam asked.

It was obvious that Wilson started to say no, then changed his mind as he remembered. "We had our bathrooms remodeled." The moment the words were out of his mouth, Wilson began to breathe more heavily, a bull pawing the ground, working himself up to attack. "Do you think someone from the crew could have—"

"We're just covering all bases," Riley interrupted him. "If you could give us the names of the people or the name of the company you hired to handle the remodeling, that would be a good start."

"Sure, right away. I've got the file in my office," Wilson said. "Lousy bastards," he cursed as he led the way down the hall.

"We're not saying they did it," Sam emphasized. Wilson didn't seem to accept anything unless he was shouted at. "But there was no sign of forced entry so unless you let them in yourselves or left a window on the ground floor opened …"

He let his voice trail off, waiting for a contradiction—or an admission of negligence. Some people still left their doors unlocked.

"Everything was closed tighter than a drum," Wilson assured them.

Reaching his office, he walked in. The condition of the room was like all the others. It had been summarily tossed in the search for valuables. Grumbling about what he wanted to do to the robbers if he ever got his hands on them, Wilson went to his desk and opened one of the drawers. It took him several minutes to find the file he was looking for.

"Here," he said, handing the file to Sam.

It was a rather thick file, Sam noted. He didn't feel like having to root around through the victim's personal papers.

"Just a business card'll do," Sam told him, handing the file back to Wilson.

Muttering under his breath, a man on his last nerve, Wilson rummaged through the file.

In the interim, Riley started to hand Shirley Wilson her card, only to stop and realize her business cards still had her old number from the homicide division. She would have to get new ones, she thought. Frustrated, she turned toward Wyatt.

"You have a card, Wyatt?" she asked, holding out her hand.

He paused to take one out of his wallet and gave it to her. She in turn handed the card to Mrs. Wilson. "If you think of anything, anything at all," she underscored, "please give us a call. Day or night." She pointed to the last line on the card. "That's my partner's number."

"Don't you have a number?" Shirley asked. She looked sheepishly at Sam, then said, "I'd rather, you know, talk to you if there's anything that comes up."

"Dial that number and ask for me," Riley told her. "My partner will transfer the call," she assured her, then added, "I don't have my cards yet."

"Oh." Shirley cast a quick, covert side glance at her husband who rifled through the file and had reached the end of his patience. "I know how that is," she said in a lowered voice.

Riley wasn't sure exactly what the woman was driving at, but she thought it best not to ask.

"Here," Wilson announced, thrusting a silver-faced business card at Wyatt. "Here's their card."

Sam glanced at it before slipping it into his pocket. "Thanks," he said. "We'll return this to you."

"Just get our things back," Wilson growled.

They remained a few more minutes, examining other rooms and trying not to get in the way of several crime scene investigators who were still there, cataloguing evidence.

When they finally left, Riley saw Sam shaking his head as they walked to his car.

"What?" she pressed. There was no way she wanted him to keep quiet when it came to the robbery. This was *their* case, not just his case. If she was going to be his partner, then she needed to know what was going on in his head.

But when he spoke, it had nothing to do with the case. "There's just another example of why I'm not married," he told her.

It had gotten pretty intense in there, but nothing she hadn't witnessed before. She'd lost count how many times she'd offered up thanks that her mother had wound up with Brian Cavanaugh and not, instead, a victim of domestic violence the way she'd been heading years ago. Granted she was a policewoman, trained to defend herself, but her father was a cop and ultimately, it came down to him being stronger.

"Not every couple bickers like that," she told Wyatt as they reached his vehicle.

"I dunno." Things, he reasoned, had a way of deteriorating and familiarity often bred contempt, not contentment. "I bet when they first got married, those two probably thought that the sun rose and set around each other."

"At least Wilson was pretty certain it did that around him," Riley couldn't help interjecting. She got into the car. When Wyatt sat behind the steering wheel, she continued. "People don't change *that* much," she maintained. "Cute little traits become annoying habits, but other than that …" Her voice trailed off and then she shrugged, thinking of what she'd just witnessed. "A jerk by any other name is still a jerk."

Sam laughed as he started up his car. "I take it you're referring to Mr. Wilson."

"He was the only jerk in the room."

He hadn't liked Wilson either, but he cut the man a little slack because of circumstances. "He'd just gotten his house robbed and had his manhood handed to him. It had to have stung his ego."

"Still no reason to take it out on his wife."

Pressing down on the accelerator, Sam made it through a yellow light. "No argument."

Riley sank into her seat, glaring straight ahead, memories crowding in her brain. She struggled to shut them out.

"My dad was like that," she said without any preamble as they flew through another yellow light. She felt Sam looking at her, but she kept her eyes front. "Always finding a reason to pick a fight." Like someone waking up from a trance, her words played themselves back to her and she glanced in Wyatt's direction, not knowing what to expect. She couldn't read his expression. He was someone she wouldn't have invited to a poker game. "We didn't have this conversation," she told him tersely.

He could respect privacy, even if it aroused his curiosity.

"What conversation?" Sam asked innocently.

They understood each other. Sort of. She nodded her head and looked straight ahead again. "Good."

"Anything else you need to say that you want to issue a disclaimer for afterward?" he asked.

"No." Shifting in her seat, the seat belt biting into her shoulder, she looked at Wyatt and said, "but I do have a question."

This time, he had to stop. There wasn't enough time to race through the amber light. He pressed down on the brake and then met her gaze.

"Shoot."

"Is this robbery really like the other case you have? I haven't had a chance to look at the file yet and thought you could give me a thumbnail sketch."

He nodded. He had no problem with that. He wasn't one of those people who felt everyone had to plow their own row. Sharing often sped things along.

"No forced entry. People are in the house, asleep," he recited. There had been four people in the house rather than just a married couple, but the basic facts were the same. "The robbers tie them up, then use chloroform on them so that they can escape without worrying about the police being summoned immediately. The garlic, though, is new," he allowed, shifting his foot back onto the accelerator.

She nodded. "You might consider going back to the first victims and asking about that detail."

"Why?" He saw no reason for something so trivial. "The robber probably ate something for dinner that had garlic in it. Even if he does that on a regular basis, it's not exactly something we can use."

"No, but what if it isn't because of something he eats?" she suggested. She saw she had his attention and went on. "Maybe when he sweats, he smells like garlic. I knew a kid in elementary school who was like that," she told him. It had been years since she'd thought of Joel Mayfield. "The kids made fun of him all the time. The sad thing was, the more fun they made of him, the worse it got."

He'd never been one to be singled out and picked on, nor had he ever picked on anyone, not even to be part of a group. Ever for the underdog, he hated people who did that.

"What happened to him?" he asked.

She thought a minute, then remembered. "His parents moved when he was ten." After that, she never heard about him again. No one she knew even wanted to stay in touch with Joel. "By now, he's either some wealthy millionaire, obsessively working his way into a fortune to show up all those kids who tormented him. Or he's a serial killer."

He nodded, understanding her reasoning. It was always people on the fringe of society that surprised the rest of the people. "For everyone's sake, I hope it's the former."

"Yeah." And then, remembering, Riley glanced at her watch. She took out her cell phone.

"Who are you calling?" he asked, making a right at the end of the next block.

She didn't answer him. The phone on the other end of the line was already ringing. "Hi, it's just me, Riley. I'm calling to check how everything's going. Uh-huh. Terrific. You know where to find me if you need to. Thanks. 'Bye." Closing the cell phone, she leaned slightly to the left to tuck it back into her pocket. She looked at him and smiled. "By the way, your daughter's doing fine."

His daughter.

God, he'd forgotten about her again. How long was it going to take for him to get used to the idea of having a child? Of being a parent? He had no answer for that.

"My daughter," he said out loud. "Do you have any idea how odd that sounds?"

"Probably as odd as having a dad seems to her," she speculated. "The only difference is Lisa will probably adjust to the concept very quickly. The same can't be said for you."

He spared her a glance, then took another right. He didn't like being typecast this way, even if there was more than a grain of truth in what she said.

"Just what makes you so certain you know me so well?" After all, they hadn't really seen each other since the academy.

"I don't," she admitted. "It's just a calculated guess on my part because you're a grown-up compared to her not being one. Kids are the resilient ones in this setup." She scanned the area. This didn't look familiar to her. "We on our way back to the precinct?"

"Nope."

Was he going to make her drag it out of him? "Then where?"

Obviously, the answer was yes. "Since you think you know me so well, you tell me."

She shook her head. She didn't like games. "You're losing the points you just gained."

"And what points would those be?"

"The points you got for sticking up for Mrs. Wilson when her husband started coming down on her."

That was business as usual for him. Realizing that the SUV in front of him was stalled, he swerved around it at the last minute.

"The woman had just been through a lot and she didn't need him needling her on top of it." He slanted a glance in her direction. "And that got me points?"

"Yeah, but don't let it go to your head," she warned. "And by the way, we're going to see the construction guy from the business card, right?"

He laughed. "Give the little lady a prize."

"I warned you about that 'little lady' stuff," she reminded him. "Okay, you're officially back to zero."

Sam laughed. He had to admit he was getting a kick out of this exchange. "Didn't take me long, did it?"

"No," she agreed, "it didn't."

And then, because she couldn't help herself, she laughed, as well. Maybe this being partnered with Wyatt wasn't going to be so bad after all.

At least not in the short run.

Chapter 7

The trip to C&R Construction turned out to be an exercise in futility. It was located clear across town in a tiny, broom-closet-sized suite that was part of a labyrinth-like, single-story industrial development.

The man who owned the company—and both of the initials, it turned out—had what he claimed was an airtight alibi for the time of the robbery. He'd been busy cheating on his wife with his mistress, a woman he'd been seeing for the last ten months. Since he spent the better part of half an hour trying to convince them jointly and then separately to make use of his professional skills, this little nugget of information took almost an hour and the threat of going to the precinct for interrogation before Calvin Richmond finally surrendered the alibi, along with his mistress's name, number and address.

"It's not that we don't believe you," Sam said, pocketing Richmond's note, "but we need to verify everything. You know how it is." His smile never wavered as he went on to ask, "What about your men?"

Richmond blinked, his dark eyebrows drawing together in consternation. "What men?"

"The ones who work for you," he replied patiently.

Richmond blew out a short breath. "Hell if I know," he grumbled.

"Where are they?" Sam asked, enunciating each word deliberately.

"Again, hell if I know," Richmond repeated, this time more defiantly.

It wasn't hard for Riley to read between the lines. "You use illegals, don't you?"

"I spread opportunity around," Richmond countered, daring her to prove anything.

"And these 'spreadees,' they have names?" Riley prodded.

Richmond raised and lowered his sloping shoulders. "They're all just willing hands to me."

Wyatt exchanged looks with her. "In other words, they're gone?" he asked.

Richmond allowed a note of exasperation to enter his voice, as if he was the victim here. "In any words, they're gone. Haven't you heard?" he asked, copping an attitude. "The economy's in a slump. People don't care about getting things upgraded if they're worried about making mortgage payments." His frustration slipped out. "Everyone's tightening their belts. What I do is considered nonessential." Holding up his thumb and forefinger, he created a tiny space between the two. "Right now, I'm this far away from declaring bankruptcy."

All the more reason to think that the man was behind the home invasions. "You sound like a desperate man," Riley observed, her eyes never leaving his.

Richmond opened his mouth to make a retort, then closed it abruptly.

Fear mingled with self-righteous indignation in his voice. "Hey, I know where you're going with this. Well, you're wrong," he declared. "I might be desperate, but not enough to break into anyone's house. That's illegal."

Wyatt moved to Richmond's other side. He and Riley now bracketed the man. "So is having people without green cards or social security numbers working for you."

"Yeah," Richmond reluctantly admitted, his small brown eyes shifting back and forth between the two detectives bedeviling him, "but I draw the line against *real* illegal stuff."

They weren't going to get any further here today, Wyatt thought. Two steps had him at the door. "We'll check out your alibi," he promised the construction company owner.

Riley lingered at the man's desk for a moment longer. "And don't try calling your girlfriend to make sure she backs you up. If you do, I promise you, we'll know," she warned ominously.

They walked out of the claustrophobic suite with Richmond, no doubt, nervously staring after them.

Wyatt waited until they were across the parking lot before saying, "Anyone ever tell you that you've got a way of unsettling a guy?"

Riley allowed a self-satisfied grin to curve her mouth. "Might have come up once or twice," she allowed, waiting for Wyatt to unlock the vehicle's doors.

Then they drove to see Richmond's girlfriend.

Thirty minutes later, after talking with Elaine Starling, a woman whose voice sounded as if she had a daily diet of helium, they got back into Wyatt's car. Elaine had verified Richmond's alibi. Of course, Riley speculated, since both robbers had been dressed in black from head to toe, the woman could have actually been Richmond's accomplice. And even if he was innocent, that still didn't rule out the men he'd had working for him on the Wilsons' bathrooms.

For now, they weren't going to get any further. Sitting back in her seat, Riley waited for her partner to start up the car again, but he paused.

When she looked at him quizzically, he said, "We're off the clock."

She glanced at her watch. "So we are."

Tired, frustrated, Wyatt rotated his shoulders. It didn't lessen the stranglehold tension had on them. "You want to go to Malone's for a drink?"

Malone's was the favorite gathering place for the Aurora detectives. At this point, it was almost a family place, except just a bit edgier.

"I'd like that," she admitted. "But you've got a kid

to pick up." She saw by the expression that entered Wyatt's eyes that she'd nudged his memory again. "You forgot again, didn't you?"

There was no point in denying it. He blew out an annoyed breath. "That's three times today. I really suck at this parenting thing, don't I?"

Was he expecting sympathy or agreement? She couldn't tell. She could only say what was on her mind. "It's just the first day, Wyatt. Cut yourself a little slack. You'll get better at it," she assured him with conviction. "Drop me off at the precinct so I can get my car," she requested. "I'll do the paperwork for today and you can go pick up your daughter."

"Aren't you coming, too?" he asked in a voice that wasn't nearly as authoritative as it had been when they were questioning Richmond.

"You don't need me to pick up your daughter. Brenda knows what you look like."

"I wasn't thinking of Brenda." He wanted her for backup. The way he saw it, this was not unlike a dangerous confrontation that could go either way.

She looked at him, surprised. "You're scared, aren't you?"

He could have bluffed, pretended that he didn't know what she was talking about. But Sam didn't see the point in pretending. "Petrified."

"She's only a little girl," Riley reminded him, her voice softening as sympathy wove through her. She remembered him asking her for help even as they left Lisa with Brenda this morning. The look on his face made her laugh. "Maybe I should rent *Sorrowful Jones* for you," she suggested whimsically.

Sam started the car and didn't have a clue what she was talking about. "What?"

"It's an old Bob Hope movie my mom and I used to watch," she told him, then went on to give him a synopsis of the simplistic plot. "A gambler leaves his little girl with a bookie as a marker in lieu of payment, promising to return right away. But something happens and he doesn't come back for her. Sorrowful is a stingy bachelor who hasn't dealt with anyone under the age of eighteen for years. He's left to figure out how to take care of the little girl until her father comes again."

He stared at her as if she'd just lost her mind. "You're kidding me."

Riley moved her head back and forth, her straight blond hair swinging softly to underscore the movement. "Things were a lot simpler back in the early fifties. Or maybe the movie took place in the forties," she told him. "I just remember there was a happy ending."

Then this was actually a movie? Someone had actually watched this? Had she? "Where do you get this stuff?"

"I told you, my mom turned me on to the classic movie channel. I like the movie," she answered with a trace of defensiveness. Straightening, she looked at Wyatt, and her defensiveness melted. "You'll be fine," she assured him.

"I'll be better if you come with me," he emphasized. "Lisa likes you. She'd feel less alienated if you're there, too."

That was when she remembered that she'd promised
Lisa to come back. It wasn't in her to refuse a child.
"You're playing dirty," she accused.

"No argument," he admitted freely, speeding up a
little as the traffic opened up. "I'm playing any way I
can to get you to say yes."

Riley was glad that there was no one to overhear
them right now because, taken out of context, it could
be misconstrued as a very loaded statement. This was
how rumors got started.

"Okay," she relented, "but you do the report tomorrow."

"Done."

"We still need to stop at the precinct," she went on,
"so I can pick up my own car." A skeptical look came
over his face. She read it correctly. "Don't trust me?"
She didn't bother waiting for him to answer. "Somebody
actually take off on you?"

He thought of Andrea. And of his mother. "Yeah."
The single word was expelled as if it had been clogging
his lungs, keeping him from breathing.

Riley stared at him. She found that almost impossible to believe. She could see him walking away
from a relationship, or what appeared to be the start
of a relationship. She couldn't see a woman suddenly
declaring that she was leaving him. Moreover, she
couldn't even see a woman quietly slipping away. The
man was mind-stoppingly handsome. But then, by
his admission, Lisa's mother had left him. "Who?"
she prodded.

Wyatt's face darkened. "That's not up for discussion."

Ordinarily, she retreated, letting people have their secrets. But in a way, this involved her. She needed to know. "It is now. Who walked out on you?" When he said nothing, she asked. "Lisa's mother?"

He stared straight ahead at the road, driving. "I already told you about that."

Riley studied his rigid profile. "But that's not who you were thinking of, was it?"

She was like a bulldog with a bone. Or a pit bull. "Ever think of using your powers for good instead of evil, McIntyre?"

"All the time," she deadpanned, then quipped, "Evil's more fun." For now, she let him keep his secret. "Okay, we're wasting time. Let's table this for now. But in case you think you're off the hook here, you're not," she assured him. "You owe me an answer." There was no room for argument in her voice.

All Sam really cared about was that she backed off. Since she had, he could pretend to go along with what she was saying. "Okay."

"And I'm going to collect." Riley sighed. "I'm serious, Wyatt."

Sam slanted a look in her direction. "It never occurred to me that you weren't."

"You know you need to take at least part of tomorrow off, don't you?" she asked just as they were approaching the precinct.

"Why?"

For an intelligent man, he was a babe in the woods when it came to his responsibilities toward his daughter.

"Because Lisa belongs in school and you need to enroll her. The sooner the better."

His only response was to groan.

"She was an absolute dream," Brenda told them less than half an hour later when they came to pick up the little girl. "Unlike my own children," she added, giving the two in question as stern a look as she could. They appeared properly subdued, an act that would likely last ten minutes. "Any time you need someone to look after her," she told Sam, "just give me a call."

"How do you feel about a permanent assignment?" Riley asked. "After school each day."

Brenda responded exactly the way Riley thought she would. "Sure, no problem. What elementary school does she attend?"

Sam was about to say that he needed to enroll the little girl when Lisa spoke up without warning. "St. Theresa's."

All three of the adults exchanged glances. "I can look it up," Riley volunteered, addressing Wyatt.

The next moment, the need for that was negated as Lisa rattled off the address. It turned out to be a local one, less than two miles away from where Sam lived. Which meant that the daughter he didn't know about had been close all this time. It was a small, small world, he concluded.

Riley ran her hand along Lisa's hair. "At least there won't be a problem with enrolling her quickly somewhere," she pointed out. "One problem down."

"And a thousand to go," Sam murmured under his breath.

To his surprise, Lisa turned around and looked up at him. "There aren't a thousand problems," she said with conviction.

Riley slipped her arm around the little girl's shoulders. "You're absolutely right. Your dad just likes to exaggerate sometimes. It helps him focus."

"What's he focusing on?"

"On what's important." Riley looked up at Wyatt. "Isn't that right, 'Dad'?" she asked pointedly, her expression telling him that she expected him to agree.

Feeling somewhat overwhelmed, Sam lost track of what she was talking about. He figured it was safe if he just shrugged his shoulders and went along with it.

"If you say so, it must be true." Before leaving, he stopped to say one last thing to Riley's stepsister-in-law. "Thanks a lot for taking Lisa on such short notice." He took out his wallet. Opening it, he drew out all the bills he had. "Look, I'm really, *really* new at this kind of thing, so I have no idea. What's the going rate for watching kids?"

Brenda shook her head, pushing his hand back toward him. "Put your money away, Detective. We'll talk about this some other time," she promised. And then she winked just before shutting the door.

The response surprised him a little. He tucked the bills into his wallet, then put the wallet into his back pocket.

"Your stepsister-in-law just winked at me," he told Riley as he quickly lengthened his stride to catch up. They reached the curb where both their vehicles were parked.

"That's just Brenda's way of saying she likes you."
It had taken her a little getting used to, but Riley kept
that to herself. She unlocked the door on the driver's side
of her car, then tossed her purse onto the passenger seat.
"She's one in a million."

Lisa moved closer to her. "May I go with you?" she
asked suddenly.

Was that relief Riley saw in Wyatt's eyes? He was
probably not looking forward to sharing the ride home
with the little girl. Conversations with a six-year-old
were probably unfamiliar to him, she guessed. Still, he
had to learn. He was the only parent Lisa had left.

"Don't you want to ride with your dad?" Riley asked
as tactfully as she could.

Lisa didn't take the hint. Like most children her age,
Wyatt's daughter was the personification of honesty.
"No, I want to ride with you," she quietly insisted.

Well, at least she doesn't throw tantrums, Riley thought.

She looked over the little girl's head at Wyatt, but the
latter seemed relieved. And Lisa gazed up at her with
pleading eyes.

Riley caved. "Fine with me."

That was all that Lisa needed to hear. Like a bullet,
the little girl raced to the passenger side of the vehicle,
pulling at the door handle.

Riley hit the lock release on the driver's armrest. The
other locks instantly popped up in unison.

"You have to ride in the back, honey," Riley told her
kindly, then turned toward her partner. She'd forgotten
about this earlier when they were coming here. "Doesn't

she have a car seat?" Lisa might be six, but she was petite and definitely under the weight cutoff point.

Wyatt started to say he didn't know, but Lisa cut in. "I do. It's at home." Lisa looked sad. "Car seats are for babies."

"And petite little girls. Trust me, you'll like that description some day," Riley said with a wink of her own. And then she replayed what Lisa had said. "Honey, if the car seat was in your mother's car, I'm afraid it's gone." The car had been totaled. "We'll have to get you another one."

Again Lisa shook her head. "Mama had another one for me. It was in the spare bedroom. In my home," she emphasized. "I've got more things there, too. Aunt Carole didn't bring everything with her when she brought me." A small, shaky sigh separated her sentences. "She just wanted me to start getting used to you," she explained, looking at Wyatt.

"I'm going to go see 'Aunt Carole' about getting a key to your mom's apartment so I can get the rest of your things," he promised.

No sooner were the words out of his mouth than Lisa dug into the tiny purse she had been carrying around and held up a key.

"Is this okay?" she asked innocently.

He took the key from her. "Is that a key to your apartment?" he asked the little girl in disbelief.

"Yes. That's why I gave it to you," she answered as if she didn't understand what the problem was.

He remembered being a lot older before his father

trusted him with a key to the house. "Aren't you a little young to have your own key?"

"No," she replied authoritatively.

Riley did her best to hide her amusement. "Guess we can't argue with that," she commented. For all they knew, the landlord was trying to rent out the apartment already. "Why don't you go over there and see about getting Lisa her things? And while you're doing that, I'll take Lisa over to your place." She looked at the little girl. "How do you feel about pizza for dinner?"

"No pepperoni," Lisa responded. "I'm not supposed to have meat."

"A miniature vegetarian," she marveled. "Okay, no pepperoni on your side," she compromised.

Wyatt struggled against feeling constricted. His first reaction to McIntyre's offer was relief. But that was wrong. This wasn't her problem, it was his and he had to face up to it sooner or later.

"You don't mind?" he asked.

"If I minded," Riley pointed out, "I wouldn't have suggested it. I don't do martyr well," she assured him, then put out her hand. "Now give me the keys to your apartment so I can get in. My B&E techniques are a little rusty."

Sam took his apartment key off his key chain and handed it to her. "I owe you."

Riley grinned and he caught himself thinking that she had the ability to light up an area with her smile. "Yeah, you do," she told him.

The next minute, she got into her car and drove off.

Chapter 8

It took Sam almost two hours before he finally returned to his own apartment.

He had trouble deciding exactly what to take and what to leave behind. He had no idea what little girls considered necessary. The two suitcases she'd brought with her had more than an adequate supply of clothing in them. But even he knew that little girls—even precocious ones—didn't live by simply clothes alone. So when he came across a somewhat misshapen teddy bear under the bed, he picked up the stuffed animal and dusted it off, tucking the toy into Lisa's car seat, which was one of the things he intended to take with him.

Sam didn't go into the apartment, or through its rooms, alone. The woman from the complex's rental office was just shutting down for the night when she saw him unlocking Andrea's door. Since she didn't recognize him and knew the circumstances surrounding her late tenant, as well as being incredibly curious, the matronly woman took it upon herself to investigate.

Accosting him as he went through the door, Mavis Patterson swiftly went from suspicious to sympathetic the moment she discovered that he was taking Lisa in and was there to pick up more of her things.

A widow for more than ten years, the heavyset woman insisted on helping him with his mission. She even brought several boxes from the rental office to help him pack up and volunteered to help carry the things he was taking to his car.

With an air of someone who had done this before, she supervised his selection.

"I like to think of everyone here as family," Mrs. Patterson told him as she trailed behind him when he made the final trip from the apartment to the car. "Some family members you can do without," she admitted, "but Andrea, she was really something else again. Always had a good word for everyone—when she stopped to talk," Mavis qualified. "Busy as all get-out most of the time." And then she switched gears as she continued her summation. "Sure was proud of that little girl of hers. Smartest thing I've ever seen. Smarter than a lot of the people living here," Mavis confided, lowering her voice.

"You need anything, you let me know," she instructed solemnly. "And not just until the end of the month, neither. Lease is up then," she informed him, "but I'm not." She patted his hand as he placed the last box into his trunk. Sam firmly shut the trunk. "Tell Lisa that Mrs. Patterson says hi."

"I'll be sure to do that," Wyatt promised.

Mrs. Patterson stood to the side as he pulled out of the covered parking slot, then watched as he drove away. She waved until he disappeared from view.

Guiding the vehicle out the apartment complex, Sam wondered if he could do anything to stall his arrival home a little longer.

The next moment, he grew annoyed with himself. Since when had he become a coward? Hell, he'd faced down armed felons. Why did the thought of coming home to his daughter suddenly send these chills shimmying up and down his spine?

His daughter.

That still didn't sound right to him. Wrapping his head around the concept of having and being responsible for a child would take him some time. A hell of a lot of time.

He glanced at his watch as he drove. Damn, Riley wasn't going to be happy about him being away for so long. Not that he blamed her.

Just what he needed. Two females to face, not just one.

He supposed it could have been worse. There could have been three of them.

It only occurred to Sam after he'd walked up to the front door of his ground floor apartment and slipped his hand into his pocket that he couldn't open the door. He had no key.

With a suppressed sigh, he realized that he had to knock on his own door in order to get in. So much for just quietly slipping inside.

He knocked. Several minutes went by. It didn't sound as if anyone stirred inside. Certainly no one was opening the door. Had Riley gone out with Lisa?

All kinds of alternate scenarios began to suggest themselves. Was this what parenthood was like? Half-formed fears chasing through his brain? He couldn't say he much cared for it.

Sam raised his hand, about to knock again, when the door finally opened.

Riley flashed him a somewhat weary smile. "I thought maybe you'd lost your way," she commented, opening the door wider to allow him to walk in.

"I had trouble deciding what she was going to need," he muttered, setting down the box he was carrying on the sofa.

Turning around to continue with his explanation, Sam faced the kitchen and saw the table. A pizza box, its bottom heavily leached with olive oil, took up nearly half of it. There was more than half a pie left. But it was the not-quite-fading aroma of the pizza that got to him, teasing awake his salivary glands.

"Did you get the car seat?" Riley was asking.

"Yes. I've got it in the car." He snapped out the answer, then told himself he had no right to lose his temper with her. Riley was doing him a favor, not the other way around. "I almost forgot it," he admitted. "Just as I was about to go into Andrea's apartment, the landlady came to check me out, probably to make sure I wasn't trying to break into the empty apartment." And then he sighed. "Once she heard that I was Lisa's father, she just wouldn't stop talking."

The corners of Riley's mouth curved in amusement. "So you're late because you couldn't decide what to bring back with you and because the landlady talked too much."

"Something like that," he mumbled.

"And being nervous about hanging around Lisa had nothing to do with dragging your feet getting back here?" Riley questioned.

He bristled at her implication—even if it was true. "What are you, trying out for the department's shrink now?"

"This whole thing has hit you right between the eyes. It's okay to be nervous. That's why I volunteered to stay with her."

He looked around. "Where is Lisa, by the way?"

"In the guest room," she replied. "Asleep." She didn't add that it took her making up two stories for the little girl before Lisa nodded off and finally fell asleep. "Poor thing's exhausted by her ordeal."

"That makes two of us," Sam admitted under his breath. Shoving his hands into his pockets, he began to move restlessly about the living room. He felt as if his back was against the wall and he didn't like it. "What am I going to do with her?" he asked helplessly, keeping his voice down as he turned to his partner.

"Love her," Riley answered very simply. "She is yours, you know. Can't go wrong when you give a kid love," she assured him, then added, "My brothers, sister and I had a very rocky childhood. But throughout it all, we knew our mother loved us with all her heart." Their father loved them in his own way, but it wasn't nearly enough to make up for the way he behaved both toward them and their mother. "In the end, that love saw us through an awful lot. It really helped smooth out some of the very rough patches we went through. Love is a very powerful, necessary emotion."

He supposed she had a point. Sam sighed. "She say anything about me?" The question was hesitantly framed. He wasn't sure if he wanted an answer.

She nodded. "She talked about you a little."

Curiosity got the better of him. "What did she say?"

Her eyes smiled first, creating a warm glow about her and, strangely enough, within him.

"Lisa said she thought you were very good-looking and that she could see why her mother 'fell' for you, I believe were the words she used." Riley laughed. "This kid of yours is pretty precocious. She's going to keep you on your toes," Riley predicted.

He didn't want a kid who kept him on his toes, who provided him with a mental challenge everywhere he turned. "That's what the cases I work on are for," he told Riley. "When I come home, all I want is to kick back and relax."

"Little kids can do that, too," Riley assured him, adding, "She's not going to require being mentally stimulated 24/7."

He had his doubts. Feeling like a man trying to cross

quicksand, he dragged his hand through his hair. "I'm going to suck at this."

"Give yourself a little credit, Wyatt. Every new dad thinks he's going to be a complete disaster when he starts out. This is all new for you." Hadn't they already been through this? She supposed that Wyatt just needed to hear it again. And maybe again after that, until it finally sank in. "You'll get used to it."

He had sincere doubts about that. Just because they had the equipment to make one, not everyone—male *or* female—was cut out to be a parent. "I don't even remember *being* a kid, much less how to treat one or relate to her."

"Practice makes perfect," Riley told him cheerfully. "Besides, this one is more adult than some of the people I know. That should make it easier for you than if you were dealing with a run-of-the-mill little kid." Not that she thought he'd have one of those. Riley patted him on the shoulder. "This time next year, you'll deny ever having this conversation and showing me your vulnerable side." She saw the uncertain expression in his eyes and grinned. "Trust me, I know. I grew up with two minimacho men. News flash," she added in a stage whisper. "There's nothing wrong with being vulnerable."

Sam still shook his head. "Not a condition I choose to be in."

"It's not always that easy, Wyatt. Sometimes, circumstances dictate otherwise," she said, thinking of how she had felt looking at her former partner's lifeless body.

It was then that she realized she hadn't thought about

Diego once this whole day, not since she came to pick up Wyatt and discovered what was keeping him from the precinct.

The realization made her feel both guilty for not thinking about him and, at the same time, hopeful. Maybe she was finally over the worst of it. Maybe, with luck, she would work her way back from the all-consuming darkness.

Without the benefit of the shrink Brian wanted her to see, she realized happily. First chance she got, she would talk to Brian and appeal his decision about her seeking therapy. She was beginning to see the light at the end of the tunnel without it.

Taking a deep, fortifying breath, she looked at her partner and asked, "Hungry?"

The question caught him off guard and he had to think about it for a second. That was when he became aware of the gnawing sensation in the pit of his stomach.

"Yeah," he told her, slowly coming around. "Yeah, I guess I am."

"Good, then have at it," she encouraged, gesturing toward the remainder of the pizza. "That's why I ordered an extra large one."

First things first. Before sitting down, he dug into his pocket for his wallet. "What do I owe you?" he asked.

"Not a thing—at least monetarily," she said, amusement dancing in her eyes. When he still took out some bills, she waved them away. "Don't worry, I can afford to spring for a pizza. Besides, you don't have to be gallant about it. This isn't exactly a date."

"A date?" he echoed.

The moment the word was out, something distant and vague inside his head began to entertain the notion. When they were attending the academy together, he and Riley had gone out a number of times, but there had always been other rookies around. It had never been a one-on-one scenario.

"Yeah, a date." Her amusement increased. The thought of dating her had obviously thrown him. "If we ever are, then I'll let you pay," she promised.

He merely nodded, struggling to place everything, including the myriad sensations swirling around inside him, into proper perspective. His thoughts, mostly unfocused, couldn't stop racing through his head. "Look, about tomorrow—"

"You take Lisa to school, introduce yourself as her dad to her teacher. Go through the motions of being normal— if you can. I'll cover for you with Barker, though I'm not looking forward to that," she had to admit.

She couldn't decide whether Barker was a good guy who just liked to growl, or an idiot who threw his weight around. But she supposed it was still early in the game for final opinions.

"We can trade," Wyatt offered, picking up a slice of pizza and putting it on a paper plate. "You take Lisa to school tomorrow and I'll cover for you with the lieutenant."

She shook her head. "Not going to happen. You need to build a relationship with your daughter and I need to show Barker that he doesn't scare me." Hopefully, the lieutenant respected people who didn't cave and wouldn't view them as a threat to his authority.

"He'll be sorry to hear that," Sam said with a quiet laugh. "He likes putting the fear of God into all his people."

"God, maybe," she allowed. "Him? No," she said as she watched Sam take a healthy bite of the pizza. "By the way, I looked through every cupboard, but all I found were paper plates."

He took another bite before answering. "That's because that's what I have. This way, when I'm finished, I can just throw them out. I'm not a big fan of having the dishes pile up in the sink."

"Then don't let them pile up in the sink," she told him simply. "You need plates, Wyatt. You have a daughter, you need plates." Since he eyed her skeptically, Riley added, "Kids need a sense of stability."

He wouldn't argue with that, just with her reasoning, which seemed a little off to him. "And having plates'll do this?"

"For openers," she said confidently. "Paper plates are transient, real plates aren't. They say 'we're staying put.'" She smiled at him. "I'll give you more tips as we go along."

Granted, she was a female, but that didn't immediately make her more qualified than he was at this. "You have any kids?"

"No." She knew where this was headed—or thought she did. "I've never been married."

"You don't need to be married to have a kid," he reminded her. "I seem to be living proof of that. But if you don't have any, what makes you think you're such an expert?"

She didn't know if he was challenging her, or just curious. The man was probably very stressed out by this sudden turn of events in his life so she gave him the benefit of the doubt.

"Easy." She smiled at him broadly. "I'm just good at everything."

"Right. I should have known." He knew her well enough to sense she was kidding. "Hey, McIntyre," he called after her as she walked into the living room and picked up her purse from the sofa.

On her way to the front door, she stopped and looked at him over her shoulder. "Yeah?"

Pushing his chair away from the table, Sam got up and crossed to her. "Thanks," he told her sincerely. "For everything."

She raised and lowered her shoulders in a careless gesture. There was no need to thank her, although she had to admit the fact that he did pleased her. "That's what partners are for."

An impulse suddenly flashed through him, so quickly and sharply that it stunned Sam. She was standing only a breath away from him. Maybe it was gratitude, or maybe it was a sudden need, but he wanted to kiss her.

Common sense prevailed and restrained him. "See you tomorrow."

Riley had absolutely no idea why there was this sudden rise of temperature within her body, why the space between them seemed to shrink without either one of them making a move. She needed fresh air, she decided. Now.

"Tomorrow," Riley echoed. Still facing him, she reached behind her and pulled the door open. The next second, she'd made her retreat. It couldn't honestly be called anything else.

He thought the noise was coming from outside.

A moment ago he'd been asleep, but the sound had spliced through the darkness in his bedroom, rousing him even as it teased his brain for identification.

What *was* that?

Propping himself up on his elbows, Sam cocked his head and listened intensely. His apartment wasn't located that far from the communal pool. It seemed like someone was always throwing a party in that general vicinity. Parties that lasted well into the night and occasionally growing progressively louder by the hour. These hot October nights had everyone wanting to cool off in the pool.

But this didn't sound like some sort of a party noise. This sounded more like someone crying. A *young* someone.

And the sound wasn't coming from outside. It was coming from inside his apartment.

Sam bolted upright.

Lisa.

He was on his feet, heading toward her bedroom before his brain properly kicked in. Before his desire to maintain distance could keep him in his room, hoping to wait her out.

His inclination was to throw open the door, but he didn't want to frighten her, so he knocked. But there was no response, even when he gently rapped on the door again. He could hear her crying.

"The hell with this," he muttered under his breath. Turning the doorknob, he eased open the guest room door.

Lisa was there, a blond, wraithlike figure lost in a double bed.

Self-preservation had him momentarily entertaining the idea of quietly backtracking out and returning to his room. The next second, Sam kicked the notion to the curb and walked into the room.

"Lisa?"

There was no response. Her heart-wrenching sobbing continued. He couldn't just leave her like this.

If you woke up a kid in the middle of a nightmare, did it have any kind of repercussions? The magnitude of the things he didn't know when it came to kids was damn near overwhelming, he thought.

Taking a breath, Sam repeated her name. When Lisa still didn't respond, he bent over the bed and lightly shook her by the shoulder. "Lisa?"

Her eyes flew open.

Startled, confused, and almost immediately embarrassed, Lisa turned her face into her pillow, struggling to stop the sobs that had besieged her. Her body shook from the effort to silence herself.

Sam sat down on the edge of the bed. "Shh," he

soothed. "It's going to be okay." He said the words to reassure himself as well as her. As gently as if he were trying to capture a snowflake in his hand, he gathered the little girl into his arms.

Frightened and still very embarrassed, Lisa attempted to resist for a moment. But the sadness was just too much for her and she gave in, melting into his embrace.

"I miss Mama," she sobbed against his shoulder.

Instinctively, he began to rock with her. "I know, honey," he said softly. "I know. But it's going to be all right."

Although, for the life of him, he didn't see how at the moment.

She clung to him and he let her. It was the least he could do.

And the most.

Sam held his daughter for a long time. Until she finally fell asleep in his arms.

Then he held her a little longer.

Chapter 9

Pulling into the driveway of the modest two-story home she owned—the house that actually owned her— Riley turned off the ignition and just sat there for a moment, trying to summon a temporary wave of strength in order to get out of the vehicle.

Beyond bone-tired, she felt as if she'd crammed a full two days into one. She took in a deep breath and blew it out again. There were only two options open to her. She would either have to learn to do with less sleep— or find a way to become twins. Too much went on in each day for her to handle everything.

Because her garage was chock full of things she'd been promising herself to sort through—another chore waiting to be tackled, she thought, less than enthused—Riley had to park her car in the driveway the last few months.

The second she got out of the vehicle, she felt him watching her. Despite the hour, she knew he was out there, waiting for her. It had become a given.

Waving her hand above her head in a general greeting, she called out, "Hi, Howard."

The front door of the house next to hers opened. Or rather, it opened wider. He'd been posted there, his door ajar, for a while now, impatiently awaiting her arrival. Howard Gray, a retired, slightly overweight mechanical engineer in his early seventies stepped out onto his porch.

He smiled in response to her greeting. He hadn't always smiled. But growing close to Riley had coaxed it out of him.

"Getting in kind of late, aren't you, Riley?" he asked.

Still tired, she decided to talk to him for a moment and crossed from her driveway to his, moving around the plum tree that separated their properties.

"Howard, what did I tell you about waiting up for me?" she asked, not bothering to hide the affection in her voice.

Howard Gray had been her neighbor ever since she'd moved in three years ago. Somewhat standoffish in the beginning, the man had eventually warmed up to her. So much so that one evening, during a display of fireworks during the Memorial Day weekend, he had told her about his son.

Egan Gray had been one of the widower's two sons, a police officer with the Aurora Police Department just like she was at the time she'd moved in. The only difference was that Egan had been gunned down when he came to the aid of a convenience store clerk who was being robbed. Egan had been off duty at the time. Struggling to come to terms with the tragedy, Howard tried to bury his sorrow and lose himself in the various collections he'd amassed. Consequently, his five-bedroom house was filled to bursting with books, magazines and long-playing record albums he'd been collecting for more years than she'd been alive—but it was all to no avail. The hurt inside him continued to grow and fester—until Riley had moved in next door. After finding out about the old man's loss, Riley took it upon herself to get Howard to come around a little. In effect, she'd adopted him, making him the grandfather she'd never known. And whenever Andrew Cavanaugh threw a party, she made it a point to invite Howard.

At first Howard would drag his feet, coming up with excuse after excuse, none of which she accepted. With time, she wore him down completely and he began to attend willingly, looking forward to the gatherings.

In addition, the former engineer had also appointed himself her guardian angel, watching over her whenever he could. In a way, she kept him linked to Egan. And it was she who'd encouraged him to mend fences with his estranged son, Ethan. The latter lived back east but flew out to visit now twice a year.

"I forget," he deadpanned in response to her question. "A man my age, you can't expect me to remember everything now, can you?"

"A man your age," Riley echoed with a dismissive

laugh. "Howard, you are one of the youngest men that I know."

He chuckled. "Does your mother know you're flirting with a man three times your age?" he asked and she could have sworn she saw a twinkle in his eye, thanks to the porch being so well lit. "All right," he announced, "now that I know you're safe, I can go to bed."

"You should have gone to bed earlier," she told him. "Staying up, waiting for me to come home, isn't good for your health, Howard."

He paused in his doorway and gave her an enigmatic smile. "On the contrary, Riley, it's very good for my health."

She knew what he was saying. Everyone needed to be connected to someone. And he was connected to her. In an odd way, it gave him a reason to get up in the morning.

Riley smiled at him. "Good night, Howard."

"Good night, Riley," he replied, then closed his door.

She waited where she was until she heard him flip his lock into place, then withdrew. By the time she was on her own front step, Riley saw the lights on Howard's first floor go out. The rest of Howard's house went dark as she let herself into her house.

And another day draws to a close, she thought as another wave of weariness swept over her.

"Heads up, you've got a third one."

A little more than two weeks had passed since her stepfather had transferred her to the robbery division. She, along with Wyatt, had caught the second of the home invasion cases on her first full day there. Consequently, she didn't have to ask what the lieutenant was talking about as she looked over her shoulder to find him planted directly behind her. Riley could feel the hairs on the back of her neck standing up—and not in a good way. She pushed away from her desk and turned around.

Questions regarding this news bulletin began to pop up, then multiply in her head, but she knew better than to ask them. That was for Wyatt to do since he was the primary on the case and Barker, she'd quickly learned, was very big on protocol and red tape. Red—if the ties he wore every day were any indication—was his favorite color and an affinity for red tape seemed to come naturally to him.

Wyatt's desk buttressed against hers so that he could look up into the lieutenant's dark eyes. Wyatt's first question was, "Same MO?"

"Yes, same MO. That's what makes it a third one," Barker replied, not sparing the sarcasm. He shifted his stony gaze in Riley's direction. "Where are we on the second one?"

We. As if the lieutenant had given them any input beyond the first bit of information that had sent them to the Wilsons. She had a feeling that he was the kind who worked his people unsparingly, then took the credit for their breakthroughs.

"'We' have questioned the Wilsons until they're sick of the sight of us. We've run down everyone they've spoken to in the last six months, including grocery clerks," she threw in, then concluded with disgust, "Nothing."

The answer obviously didn't please him. "Well, see

if you can come up with 'something' this time, McIntyre," the lieutenant said in a patronizing tone. He handed Wyatt the names and address of the home invaders' newest victims. "The mayor doesn't like unsolved crimes on the books."

"He's not the only one," she muttered under her breath as the lieutenant made his way back to his office.

Sam was already on his feet, slipping on his sports jacket. "Ready?" he asked.

"As I'll ever be," she responded, pushing back her chair a little farther. She grabbed her jacket and her shoulder bag, hurrying to catch up with him.

"Coming over tonight?" Sam asked her as they passed several detectives on their way out of the squad room.

One of them, Alex Sung, looked up. A twelve-year veteran of the division, there was mild surprise registered on his face as he looked from Wyatt to Riley and then back again.

"It's not what you think," Riley told the older man flippantly. "I'm helping him study for his citizenship test."

Sung's partner, Reed Allen, stared at Wyatt, confusion on his face. "You're not a citizen, Wyatt?" he asked uncertainly.

Wyatt blew out an annoyed breath. "Don't pay any attention to her," he advised. "Somewhere a village is looking for its idiot."

"Then we have somewhere to send your next job application," she countered cheerfully.

"Overdid that a little, don't you think?" Wyatt asked her when they were outside the squad room.

Her eyes widened in deliberate innocence. "Oh, you thought I was kidding?"

He laughed shortly, shaking his head.

Pressing for the elevator, Sam found that the car was already on their floor when the elevator opened its doors.

"With you," Sam said honestly, getting in, "I can never really tell."

She liked that. It meant she was keeping him on his toes. Off balance. That leveled the playing field for her. Because something about him definitely threw her off balance.

"To answer your question, yes, I can come over." The elevator closed its doors again. She pressed for the first floor. "Lisa asking for me?"

He nodded. "Every morning." While he was relieved to be sharing the responsibility, he had to admit that it did bother him a little that Lisa apparently preferred McIntyre to him.

"Eventually, you know, you're going to have to fly solo," she told him as the doors opened again. They got off and walked toward the front of the building. "Spend the morning *and* the evening with her without a go-between getting into the mix somewhere."

"I'll cross that bridge when I come to it," he replied vaguely. Reaching the front door, he opened it for her, then checked the address on the paper that Barker had given him. "Same part of town as the other two, except this one's a little closer to the center than the last one."

"Maybe the invaders are getting more democratic in their choice of victims," she cracked. Assuming that he would want to drive, she headed toward where he usually parked his vehicle.

"Sure would be nice to find that they had something more in common than just geography," Sam commented. He automatically slipped his hand into his pocket, feeling around for his car keys.

"We will," she promised.

Sam unlocked the door on her side. All the locks released at the same time. "I'm not as optimistic as you are," he told her, rounding the trunk and coming around to his side.

She got into the car. "I noticed. But we'll find it. Maybe even this time around," she added.

So far they'd established that the two couples didn't know each other and had nothing in common except for living in a house valued in the millions. Beyond that, there seemed to be no common denominator.

Early that morning, Riley had run down the list of information they'd compiled for what seemed like the umpteenth time. The first victims, Edith and Joel Marston, attended church services every Sunday, the Wilsons didn't. The Marstons had two children under the age of eighteen who went to private schools, the Wilsons were childless. The Marstons took three vacations a year. Mr. Wilson was a workaholic and he and his wife hadn't been away in close to three years. Mrs. Wilson went to the gym at least four times a week. The Marstons didn't have a gym membership.

And so it went. The two couples' paths didn't cross—

except that they had to, she thought as they drove to the home of the third victims. Someway, somehow, the paths *had* to cross.

The third home invasion victim was John Cahil, a divorced college professor and the father of two teenaged sons, neither of whom were with him at the time the invasion went down. His girlfriend of ten months wasn't as fortunate. After dining at their favorite restaurant, John Cahil and his girlfriend, Rhonda Williams, came back to his home, made love while inebriated and fell asleep in his California King-sized bed.

That was where they were, sound asleep in his bedroom, when the two black-clad robbers struck.

According to the information gathered by the first officer on the scene, the MO was identical to the other two robberies. With one slight difference. This time, one of the robbers, the smaller of the two, had lingered over Rhonda, who became hysterical. Despite being tied up, John had voiced his protest, calling the robber several unflattering names. He'd succeeded in diverting the threat away from Rhonda because the robber had beaten him for his stab at chivalry. His accomplice had been forced to pull him off the professor and angrily told him to remember what they had come for.

Other than that, everything went according to the old plan. The victims had been tied up, their mouths and limbs duct-taped and just before the ordeal was over, they were chloroformed.

When Riley and Wyatt arrived, the professor and his girlfriend were twelve hours into their ordeal. Other than the hours that she'd been unconscious, Rhonda looked as if she'd been crying for most of that time.

After introducing himself and Riley, and extending his sympathy and condolences for what they had been through, Sam asked them to please recount the events that occurred after the robbers had woken them up in the bedroom.

Outraged, the professor flatly refused to talk about it "again." "I've already told that officer everything that happened. You want to know, talk to him," Cahil snapped. Putting his arms around Rhonda, he tried to console her. She continued sobbing into the handkerchief he'd given her. By now, it was crumpled and soggy.

"Professor, we're hoping that you might remember something if you tell it again, something you forgot the first time around," Riley said, hoping to appeal to his softer side. "Even the smallest thing might help us finally get these people."

His gray eyes seemed to flash as he looked up at them. "I know the statistics for success in these things and they're dishearteningly low," he snapped at them. "I teach criminology, for God's sake." The statement was accompanied by self-depreciative laughter.

Riley exchanged looks with her partner. Had the experience of actually being the victim of a robbery made the professor go off the deep end?

"There's irony for you," Cahil announced bitterly,

still holding Rhonda. "The professor of criminology is a victim of a crime."

Sniffling, Rhonda gazed up at him. It was obvious that she was desperately trying to pull herself together—and move forward in a positive manner.

"John, calm down," Rhonda pleaded. She tried to soothe him by placing her hand on his arm, but he shook her off. Suddenly, their roles were reversed and it was she who was trying to comfort the professor.

From where Riley stood, the effort was doomed to failure.

"I don't *want* to calm down," he retorted with passion. "I want those two bastards dead and these two out of my house." The professor waved his hand at Riley and her partner, then glanced toward the bedroom. Commotion still came from within the room. "Along with all their unnecessary cronies."

"Those 'cronies' are very necessary, Professor," Wyatt assured him patiently. "I think you know that. And we'll be gone as soon as you give us your statement," he promised.

Tall, with gaunt features, the professor drew himself up and gave the impression of an annoyed creature of the night. "I was robbed, end of story."

"Oh, I think there's a little more to the story than that," Riley speculated, doing her best to sound sympathetic. She looked directly at the bruises on his face. "You did something to make at least one of them mad at you. What did you do?"

"Nothing." The single word effectively withdrew

him completely from the people who were in the room. Riley had a feeling the man was one hard-nosed educator. No curves when it came to grades in his class, she mused.

It was Rhonda who gave them their answer. "He stood up for me."

"Rhonda." There was a warning note in the professor's voice.

Well, at least he wasn't a man who liked to be in the center of things and draw attention to himself, Riley thought.

"Well, you did." Rhonda shifted and eyed the two detectives. "His own hands were tied up and everything, but Johnny still tried to get that awful creep to take his hands away from me."

"Very brave of you, Professor." Riley'd almost called him "Johnny" as well, but stopped herself just in time.

He shrugged off the compliment. "Yes, well, didn't get me very far, did it?" the professor grumbled.

Riley turned toward Wyatt. "May I see you for a second?" she asked.

Impatient, Wyatt excused himself from the two victims and stepped out of the room with Riley.

"What's up?" he asked. It wasn't customary to back away before an interview was over and as far as he was concerned, it wasn't over.

"Why don't you take the professor aside and question him by yourself? Without me or his girlfriend around," she suggested, keeping her voice low. "He might open up to another man." And then she smiled at him. "You know how fragile the male ego is."

"Not personally," he replied. "But that's not a bad idea, McIntyre," he said, nodding his head. "It's worth a try. Without him around, his girlfriend might feel more comfortable about telling you exactly what happened."

"Might," Riley agreed.

"Let's give it a shot," Sam said just before he crossed back into the living room.

New plan in place, they proceeded to divide and, with any luck, conquer.

Bringing the two victims together again, Riley and Sam were on the verge of wrapping up the interview when Rhonda commented to Cahil that Anna and Ellen would be in for a surprise tomorrow.

"Anna and Ellen?" Wyatt repeated. "Who are they and why are they going to be surprised?"

"Anna's my maid," Cahil answered. "Ellen's her daughter. They come in twice a week to clean my house. I don't see how that has anything to do with this." A private man, he resented having his life dissected this way. And then his eyes widened as he followed the train of thought he was sure was going through the detectives' minds. "It wasn't them," he said with feeling. "Weren't you listening? I said that those were men here last night, not women."

Sam made no comment on the professor's defense. Instead, he asked, "Do either Anna or Ellen have the key to your house?"

"Of course they have a key," was the exasperated answer. "How else are they going to get in here when I'm at the university? Through the chimney?"

"Works for Santa Claus," Riley quipped. It earned her a dark look from the professor.

Fear obviously trumped loyalty in Rhonda's eyes. Growing excited, she asked, "Do you think that was it? They gave the key to someone?"

"It's a possibility," Riley allowed. "We have to check it out. Until then," she continued as she looked at Cahil to emphasize her point, "they're innocent until proven otherwise. We'll need to get in contact with them."

Cahil grudgingly gave them Anna's phone number.

It was time to go. "Thank you, Professor Cahil, Ms. Williams," Sam said, calling an end to the interview. "We'll be getting back to you in the next few days," he promised.

With that, he placed his hand on the small of Riley's back, ushering her out of the room and toward the front door.

Behind them, they heard Professor Cahil snort. "I won't hold my breath."

There were days, Riley thought as she crossed the threshold, when protecting and serving turned out to be harder than others.

Chapter 10

Riley quickly discovered that, as in almost every department of the police force, man power in the robbery division was limited. She and Wyatt, along with the other detectives in Robbery, didn't lack for cases to work on. But due to the publicity that the home invasion cases had garnered and the fact that there were now three of them, they had gone to the top of the priority list.

Day in, day out, despite the fact that they sacrificed their lunchtimes and pored over the same evidence until they could re-create the reports from memory, the cases seemed to taunt them. They were still missing something.

Riley had a feeling that the solution was hiding in plain sight. She just couldn't grab onto it. Yet. It was only a matter of time before that one crucial piece of evidence would hit them. She just had to be patient.

"I must've been over all the details a hundred times," Sam complained, tossing down the folder he'd been looking through. With a deep, impatient sigh, he rocked back in his chair, staring at the bulletin board. Looking to find what he'd missed before.

Almost everything in the folders he'd put together matched, in some fashion, the abbreviated notes on the board they'd put up next to their desks.

But so far, there'd been no breakthroughs. The professor's cleaning ladies turned out to be just that: cleaning ladies. A background check on both women connected them to only one unsavory character. Anna's nephew, Jorge. But Jorge was currently doing time for almost beating someone to death who'd had the misfortune of looking at his wife. That ruled him out. In addition, a quick review of Jorge's history showed that he didn't have the kind of pull to get others to work for him and he definitely didn't have the smarts needed to run that kind of operation from his jail cell.

The other two families didn't employ any sort of cleaning service.

"You say something?" Riley asked, hearing Wyatt mutter something inaudible under his breath.

He glanced up at her. "Yeah. This running around in circles is getting to me."

That made two of them, she thought. "We need to unwind," she agreed. "Both of us," she emphasized with a sigh.

"Good luck with that." He looked accusingly at the piles on his desk, but he was too brain weary for the moment to pick up another folder.

It was Friday and it was late. He should be going home. But even that didn't mean he could unwind. Ever since Lisa had come into his life, he didn't even stop at Malone's. Alcohol might make his brain fuzzy just when he had to be sharp.

He closed his eyes for a moment. This parenting business weighed heavily on his shoulders.

"I'm surprised the lieutenant doesn't have us working overtime," he said. Whatever extra time he and McIntyre devoted to this was off the books and on their own time. "Barker did say that the mayor was really pressing to get these invasions cleared and off the books."

Riley didn't want to hear about official overtime. That meant having to put in a mandatory number of hours and this was already nagging her brain. "A tired mind doesn't operate at maximum efficiency," she pointed out.

He laughed shortly. "You thinking of having that embroidered on your towels, or just your T-shirt?" Wyatt asked.

"Just stating the obvious." Riley paused for a moment, looking at him, debating whether or not to say what had been buzzing around in her head for the last half hour.

The pensive expression on her face was not lost on him. Lately, he noted, especially when he was tired, he caught himself watching her more often than he should. Watching her and having thoughts that went beyond the realm of their professional partnership. Right now, he wished Evans was back—or that McIntyre wasn't so damn attractive.

"Something on your mind, McIntyre?" he asked.

Rather than say yes, she asked him a question of her own. "You like barbecued food?"

He stared at her. That wasn't what he'd expected her to ask. Actually, he wasn't really certain *what* he expected her to say. He'd just vaguely thought it would have to do with one of the cases. There were times when his partner's mind seemed to slip into an alternate universe.

"Well, do you?" she pressed when he didn't say anything.

"Yeah, I've been known to like barbecued food." Why was she asking him what he liked to eat? "McIntyre, are you asking me out on a date?" He splayed his hand against his chest, feigning surprise. "This is so sudden."

"It's not sudden, it's nonexistent," she informed him. "I'm just debating inviting you over to Andrew Cavanaugh's place tomorrow. You and Lisa," she added, realizing that she'd omitted that important piece of information. "By the way, Lisa's the only reason I'm even thinking about this invitation."

He thought of baiting her but was too tired to follow it through. "What's tomorrow?"

"Saturday," she answered glibly.

"I know it's Saturday." He tried not to sound exasperated. It wasn't Riley's fault he wasn't sleeping much at night, lying there listening for the sound of Lisa crying again. So far, except for that first night, the little girl hadn't. But that didn't mean she wouldn't again. If she did, he didn't want her to go uncomforted. "I mean why's the chief having a barbecue?"

"Because he can," she answered glibly, adding, "Because he likes to cook and because he *really* likes having family around to eat what he cooks. Technically, there's no occasion, but it's been so hot lately that he decided to take advantage of the weather."

He'd stopped listening at the end of the second sentence. "Only one problem with that. I'm not family," Sam pointed out in response to the eyebrow she lifted quizzically.

"You're a cop, that makes you family in the Chief's eyes. His mantra, not mine," she added in case Wyatt wanted to demur. "C'mon, what d'you say, Wyatt? There'll be great food, great conversation. Lisa can play with the gaggle of kids who'll be there and you'll get a chance to unwind."

He had to admit he was sorely tempted. Socializing had died by the wayside ever since he'd taken on the mantle of fatherhood. After hours, McIntyre was the only one he socialized with and both of them focused on Lisa.

"I've heard about these parties the Chief throws," he confessed. The food, he'd heard, was out of this world.

She laughed softly. "You'd have to live in another state in order not to hear about them. His hospitality— and culinary abilities—are famous." She looked at her partner. "So, how about it?"

He was already won over, but because it was Riley, he played it out a little longer. "I don't know. What time does it start?"

Riley grinned triumphantly. She knew she could wear him down. She wasn't about to explore why she felt this little thrill in the pit of her stomach.

"Starts at noon, goes on forever. Or at least until everyone's too tired to talk."

A whimsical smile played on his lips. "That include you?"

For a while there, because of what had happened to Sanchez, she hadn't been herself. But now Riley felt as if she was coming around again. Coming back from a dark mind-set she wouldn't have wished on anyone. The relief she experienced was incredible.

"Sometimes," she allowed.

"All right," he agreed, then qualified his reason for going. "I think you're right. Lisa might get a kick out of it."

"Of course I'm right," she said glibly. "I can swing by tomorrow, pick you up."

"Or you can just give me the address now."

Riley made no effort to reach for a piece of paper to write the address down. "That won't assure me that you'll come," she told Wyatt bluntly.

"Scout's honor carry any weight with you?" he asked archly.

"It would—if you'd been a Boy Scout," she told him with a knowing smile. "But you weren't."

"How would you know that?" Sam asked, then

realized the answer. "Have you been digging into my background, McIntyre?"

"Maybe a little," she admitted. There was no embarrassment, no apology in her voice.

Why would she go through the trouble? Was there something going on he wasn't aware of? An investigation came to mind, but there was no reason for one.

"But you know me," Sam protested.

She gave him what passed as a mysterious smile. "Does anyone really know anyone?"

The sigh that escaped was an impatient one. "Don't go all philosophical on me, McIntyre. Why were you digging into my background?"

"Because I don't like surprises. Because I wanted to know more about the man I'd been partnered with. Besides, it's not digging, it's just familiarizing myself with some background information."

Had she talked to someone, or just looked at his personnel file? In either case, he couldn't say he liked the invasion. "Asking me would have been simpler."

"Would you have answered?" she challenged.

"Maybe." His expression gave nothing away. "If you'd played your cards right," he added.

Yeah, right. "That's what I thought," she said out loud. "My way's better. Anyway, I wasn't going for any deep, dark secrets—"

"Good," he said, cutting her off. "Because I haven't got any."

Everyone had secrets, Riley thought. Some just had more or bigger ones than others. "—I just wanted to

satisfy my curiosity," she concluded as if he hadn't interrupted her.

Riley leaned back in her chair, unconsciously rotating
her shoulders to get rid of the cramp in her muscles. He
looked up and saw her moving her head from left to
right. It was a familiar movement that he'd seen boxers
employ just before a bout was about to begin.

"Getting ready for a main event?" he asked her,
amused.

"Just trying to get rid of this crick in my neck."

"That's what you get for hunching over your desk."

She hadn't noticed that Wyatt was observing her. Most
of the time, she thought he was oblivious of her presence.
"I didn't know posture counted in the robbery division."

"Everything counts in the robbery division," he said
flippantly, getting up. He circled behind her.

She turned in her chair, trying to see where he was
going. To her surprise, Wyatt righted her chair to keep
her from facing him. "What are you doing?"

"Getting ready to strangle you and I'd rather do it
from behind so those big blue eyes of yours don't get to
me," he cracked as he put his hands on her shoulders. She
jumped in response and he laughed. "Easy, McIntyre, I
was only kidding about strangling you. I thought I'd try
to help you work out those kinks." As he began to knead,
he found that he had to use excessive pressure. "Damn,
but you're tense," he commented, pressing harder. "This
is what the Hulk must feel like after he goes green and
winds up erupting out of his clothes."

Lovely, he was comparing her to a lumpy, angry

green comic book character. "Sure know how to turn a girl's head, don't you, Wyatt?"

"I don't think of you as a girl, McIntyre."

It was a lie, but a necessary one, he felt. Necessary because in reality he thought of her as a woman far too much for either of their good. Doing so interfered in so many different ways that it boggled the mind.

"Good to know," she murmured. She caught her breath, trying not to make any whimpering sounds. Wyatt was using way too much force kneading her shoulders, but she'd be damned if she'd give him the satisfaction of wincing. Instead, she tried to concentrate on something else. "You really think that I've got big blue eyes?"

Still working her shoulders, he leaned over and peered at her face. "Don't you?"

"Yes." She sat up a little straighter. The pain now shot to the top of her skull and the very roots of her hair. "But my other partners never noticed."

He sincerely doubted that. "Trust me, unless they needed a seeing eye dog to get around, they noticed."

Despite the fact that his rock-hard fingers created their own wave of pain with each pass of his hands, the stiffness in her shoulders seemed to abate somewhat. She felt almost human.

A sigh escaped her lips as she allowed herself to enjoy the sensation.

The moment was short-lived.

The phone on her desk rang. She glanced up at the clock on the wall. It was five-thirty. Thirty minutes past the end of their shift. If she picked up the phone and it turned out to be an official call, she might not go home for a while yet.

Wyatt withdrew his hands from her shoulders. "Are you going to answer that?" he asked.

"I was hoping to outlast it," she confessed with a sigh. Resigned, she picked up the receiver and put it to her ear. "McIntyre."

"Just me, honey. I tried calling your cell, but I think you let the battery wind down again. Anyway," the soft, familiar voice on the other end continued, "I'm calling to remind you about Andrew's barbecue. It's tomorrow."

She relaxed in her chair. No emergencies, no robbery to follow up on. "I was just talking about it."

"Oh?" Lila Cavanaugh made no attempt to hide her piqued interest. "To whom?"

"My partner, Mom." She watched as Wyatt went back to his desk and closed down his computer. "I invited him and his daughter. I didn't think Andrew would mind."

"Mind?" Lila echoed with a soft laugh. "You know Andrew, the more the merrier. So tell me, how's your partner adjusting to fatherhood?"

The question didn't surprise her. Even though she hadn't said a word about this new state of affairs that Wyatt found himself facing, she knew that word in her family traveled like the flames of a wildfire during the state's dry season. Brenda knew and that was enough. All for one and one for all wasn't just a slogan for a band of fictional Musketeers, it also seemed to be the Cavanaugh/McIntyre family's slogan, as well. What one knew, they all knew.

The price one paid for having them all there for you, she thought philosophically.

"Slowly, Mom, slowly." She tried to avoid looking at Wyatt, but it couldn't be helped. He had to know she was talking about him. "But he's getting there. Gotta go. See you tomorrow."

"I'm looking forward to it, honey," her mother said. "And Riley?"

She'd almost replaced the receiver when she heard her mother say her name. She snatched it up just before it connected with the cradle. "Yes?"

Her mother's warm voice embraced her. "I love you."

Riley knew her mother was still worried about her, worried that she wouldn't be able to pull out of the tailspin she'd found herself in right after Sanchez had been murdered. But, mercifully—maybe it was the work or maybe it was because she was helping out with Lisa—she seemed to be finally getting her act together.

"Me, too, Mom," she said quietly. With that, Riley hung up.

Sam waited until she replaced the receiver. "Everything okay on the home front?"

Nodding, she did her best to sound casual. "Just my mother, checking up on me."

"She have reason to worry?" he asked mildly, watching her face carefully.

"No."

The answer came out automatically, without thought so that she wouldn't be subjected to probing questions. But this time around, Riley realized there was more truth to it than just a few weeks ago. Progress. It felt good.

"But that doesn't stop her. Parents, according to my mother, worry about their kids for roughly the first hundred years. After that," she smiled, "they start to back off."

"That means you've got more than seventy years to go," he deadpanned.

Even if her life span and her mother's went that far, her mother would never completely stop worrying about them. It was an occupational hazard and the fact that all of them were on the police force didn't help matters.

"Something like that," she agreed.

"If that's what parenting's about, I'm glad I'm not like that," he told her.

There was humor in her eyes, as if telling him he would wind up eating his words. "Give yourself time. You will be. The best parents always worry, they just don't show it."

He made no comment. The thing of it was, he had this undercurrent of fear that Riley was right.

The next day, responding to the doorbell, Sam stared at the woman on his doorstep. Riley. He thought they'd settled this last night. Did she think he needed a keeper?

"You know, you didn't have to stop by. I told you that we were going to attend." He stood there looking at her, his body blocking the entrance to his apartment.

"Just wanted to be sure," she answered cheerfully. "Besides, I'm not going out of my way stopping here. I pass right by your complex when I go to Andrew's house." It wasn't entirely true, but close enough.

Riley shoved her hands into the back pockets of her denim shorts. Her very short denim shorts, Sam noted, his eyes sweeping over her. His partner wore a white halter top that emphasized her tan, but it was the shorts that really captured his attention as well as stimulated his imagination. He took slow inventory of her legs.

Who knew they were that long?

She could almost feel his eyes trailing along her body. Making her warmer. She did her best to sound blasé.

"Careful, Wyatt," she warned. "You're in danger of having your eyes fall out of your head."

"Your legs always been that long?" he asked, forcing his gaze back up to her face.

Riley looked down, pretending to take his question seriously. "Since the sixth grade. I was the tallest in my class until everyone else caught up. One of the guys used to call me Flamingo Legs."

His thoughts turned to Lisa. Someday, maybe soon, some little boy would be teasing her. How was she going to handle that? How was *he* going to handle that? He didn't want to be one of those overbearing fathers, but he knew he wouldn't like the idea of someone tormenting his daughter.

"Did it hurt?" he asked.

She grinned broadly. "No, but he did after I gave him a fat lip."

He laughed. She'd been tough even then, fighting her own battles. Maybe Lisa would be, too. "Why doesn't that surprise me?"

She couldn't pinpoint exactly why, but the sound of Wyatt's laughter shimmied up and down her spine, making her feel even warmer than the day warranted.

It also brought out his daughter from her room. Dressed in a red T-shirt and white shorts, Lisa came running up to her the moment she saw who it was.

"Riley, Riley, Sam and I are going to a barbecue," she announced.

Riley looked quizzically at Wyatt. Why was he still letting his daughter call him by his first name? "I know, honey. I invited you."

Lisa fairly danced from foot to foot. "You're going, too?" she squealed, then threw her small arms as far around Riley's hips as her arms could reach.

"You bet." Riley glanced toward her partner. "She still calls you Sam?" she asked, trying not to sound as if she had an opinion one way or the other.

Sam shrugged. "Easier to get used to than 'Dad,'" he told her.

"Same amount of letters," Riley pointed out.

"Yeah, well…" He let his voice trail off, then gazed down at his daughter. It wasn't a matter of letters, but of feelings. He'd been missing for the first years of her life. Getting used to being here with him was hard enough for her without thinking of him as her father. "C'mon, Lisa, let's get this show on the road."

He didn't have to tell her twice. Grabbing Riley's hand, Lisa fairly raced across the threshold, excitement apparently bubbling through her as she giggled.

Chapter 11

"Hear that?"

It was several hours later when Riley asked Sam the question.

When they'd arrived at Andrew's house, the barbecue was already in full swing and they were quickly embraced and then absorbed. Within minutes, Lisa had been "borrowed" from Sam. Clasping Brenda by the hand, the little girl was happily led away to join in a series of games that Brenda, Jared's wife, Maren, and Troy's wife, Delene, were overseeing, playing with the up and coming next generation of Cavanaughs. Lisa hadn't been back since.

In the interim, separately and together, Riley and Sam were drawn into one conversation after another.

The topics were varied, some serious, some humorous, but they were all spirited. Time, offset with an ever-changing array of snacks, appetizers and main meals, passed very quickly.

And now, the "official" barbecue foods—hot dogs, hamburgers and steaks—were being served. No one, even the most stuffed of them, could find it in their hearts to say no. It was all just too good. Sam had volunteered to get her serving and his, returning with both after ten minutes.

Sam handed his partner the plate Andrew had insisted on preparing for Riley himself.

"Hear what?" he asked, sitting down with his own plate on one of the dozens of folding chairs. It was nothing short of a balancing act, trying to keep everything on the extra-large paper plate rather than it come sliding onto his lap. Besides the hamburger, there were three kinds of salad, all vying for a limited amount of space. "With all this noise, it's hard to hear just one thing."

"*Listen,*" Riley underscored.

Humoring Riley, Sam cocked his head the way she was doing. He heard a lot of things, but nothing in particular. "So what am I listening for?" he asked.

Riley sighed. Men. "The sound of your daughter, laughing."

Sam straightened his head and looked at her. "You're kidding, right?" When she didn't say yes, he realized she was being serious. "You can actually hear that?" he marveled. "Lisa laughing?"

"Yes."

He listened again, then shook his head. Riley had to be pulling his leg. "There's got to be at least a dozen kids laughing, maybe more." Not to mention the countless high-pitched voices raised, competing with one another. "How can you possibly make her out?"

"I can," she insisted. "It's a matter of concentration. And attachment," she emphasized. "You're her dad, Wyatt, you are supposed to be able to tell the difference."

"Sorry," he quipped. "My 'dad' gene is a newly acquired one. It's going to take me some time to hone it properly."

Riley watched her partner for a long moment, gauging his tone. "You're making fun of me, aren't you, Wyatt?"

He pretended to be incredulous. "In a yard filled with your relatives, most of whom have access to guns?" He took a bite out of the hamburger. Damn if it wasn't heaven on a bun. How could a simple hamburger taste this good? "Wouldn't dream of it. I don't have a death wish," he assured her before he took another bite.

His comment made Riley look around for a second. As she did, she smiled to herself. She hadn't thought about it in those terms. But Wyatt was right. This *was* a yard full of her relatives.

Not blood relatives except for Taylor, Frank and Zack, and of course her mother, but one way or another, this really was her family now. And, no doubt, every last one of them would back her up whenever she needed it.

She hadn't realized how good that felt until this moment.

"You'd have to do something pretty terrible for them to shoot you," she quipped.

Swallowing another bite, Sam shook his head. "That's one envelope I have no desire in pushing."

"Oh? And what envelope would you like to push?"

Their eyes met and held for longer than she'd intended. Long enough to evoke that strange, funny shiver that danced along her spine these days whenever their hands accidentally brushed or she encountered him when she wasn't expecting to.

A strange, funny, *warm* shiver that spread out tributaries and left her stomach unsettled.

"I'll let you know when the time comes," he promised her quietly. So quietly that she had to look at his lips in order to have the words register completely.

"Oh. Okay." She went back to watching Lisa. Somehow, it seemed safer that way. And better for her digestion.

Watching Riley and her partner from across the yard, Lila smiled to herself.

A sense of relief intensified. The same relief that had begun when she first greeted Riley as she arrived with Sam and his daughter. Lila turned toward her husband, the man she could now freely admit she loved. The man who she'd loved in secret for so many years. Lila placed her hand on his arm.

"You did good, Brian," she praised in a soft, lowered voice.

"Of course I did," Brian replied, turning toward her.

Andrew had recruited him to bring another box of buns over to the grill, but that could wait. What his wife was saying intrigued him. "But just for edification purposes, is this in reference to anything specific or is this a general seal of approval?"

With a laugh, she shook her head. "Yes, it's specific. I'm talking about taking Riley out of Homicide and partnering her up with Sam Wyatt in Robbery. Look at her." Lila nodded in her daughter's direction. "She almost looks like her old self again." Lila turned toward Brian again and brushed a kiss against his cheek. "Thank you."

He took her hand and brought it to his lips, pressing a kiss against her knuckles. "No thanks necessary, milady. I'm always at the ready and at your service."

A little sigh of contentment escaped Lila's lips. After all these years, she was finally, blissfully, happy. And she owed it all to Brian.

"Nice to know," she murmured.

"I can show you just how ready I am once we get a chance to slip away and go home," he promised her with a wink.

"Brian," she laughed, glancing around to see if anyone had heard him. "You're the Chief of Detectives, don't let anyone overhear you."

"Why?" He grinned. "Where is it written that the Chief of Ds is supposed to be a robot? Or live by the letter of the law alone?" he challenged playfully. "Besides," he said, lowering his voice and whispering in her ear, "even a robot would find his mighty tin body getting overheated just by being so close to you."

She laughed again, shaking her head. It never occurred to her that she could be so happy. After what she'd gone through with her first husband, it was like living in a dream. One from which she hoped she'd never wake up.

"In my considered opinion, I'd say that Lisa is officially worn out," Riley told her partner, inclining her head close to his so that Sam could hear her.

It was almost ten o'clock and Riley's description could have fit almost any one of them—except for Andrew who seemed to literally thrive on spending hours cooking for his family and friends.

When Sam looked at her, Riley indicated the sleeping child on her lap. A number of them had adjourned to the family room and she had commandeered the corner of one of the sofas for herself and Lisa. Lisa's head now rested against Riley's chest and the little girl was curled up into her. Somewhere in the last half hour, Sam's daughter had grown progressively more and more subdued, then, after protesting that she was wide awake, had fallen asleep.

"Here, I'll take her," he said, slipping his arms around his daughter and lifting her into his arms. "Never saw her fall asleep without a fight before," he commented with a touch of amusement.

Riley glanced at the few children still milling around. Most were asleep, like Lisa, resting securely in one of their parents' arms.

"This group'll do that to you, tire you out until there

isn't an ounce of energy left inside your body," she told him, a fond smile curving her mouth as she remembered. "My brothers, sister and I were exactly the same way."

Sam nodded. "I wouldn't know about things like that, I didn't have any siblings."

Riley thought of what her childhood would have been like without her siblings. Achingly lonely.

"I'm sorry."

Curiosity entered his eyes. "Why are you sorry?" He didn't see being an only child as missing out on anything. His mother had walked out on his father when Sam was young and *that* had hurt, but being an only child hadn't. "It's not like I didn't have enough to eat."

She saw it differently. "In a way, yes. You were deprived."

The shrug was careless in nature. "You don't miss what you don't have."

But Riley shook her head. "I don't think that's absolutely true."

The woman was something else, he thought, amused. "You'd argue with God, wouldn't you?"

The smile came into her eyes as she considered his question. "Depends on what point of view He was advancing."

Sam just laughed and shook his head. "Look, I hate to drag you away from this, but since you insisted on being my ride today—"

She was on her feet, ready to leave before he could finish his sentence.

"Don't say another word," she told him. "Of course

I'll take you and Sleeping Beauty here home." She looked around, trying to locate their hosts. "Just let me find either Andrew or Rose and make our goodbyes."

He had no intentions of leaving without doing the same. "You implying I'm not capable of saying my own goodbyes, McIntyre?"

She knew she had a tendency to take charge, especially when it came to the family. She would have to watch that, Riley told herself.

"Never even crossed my mind," she deadpanned, holding up her hand as if taking a solemn pledge.

With a chorus of goodbyes still ringing in her ears and a feeling of both contentment and unexpected anticipation, Riley drove her partner and his daughter the short distance home.

"You know," he pointed out again, "if you'd have let me drive to the barbecue in my own car, you could still be back there."

"Gaining more weight?" she speculated. "No, this is the right cutoff point," Riley assured him. "You were just my excuse for leaving before I put on another five pounds. In case you haven't noticed," she went on, squeaking through an amber light, "it's hard saying 'no' to Andrew, especially when the food he's trying to push on you tastes so good."

"I noticed."

I also noticed a lot of other things better left unsaid, he thought, covertly watching her profile as she spoke.

The close proximity had him entertaining thoughts that had no business coming up. He and McIntyre were partners. They worked together and needed clear heads and lives that weren't tangled up with one another's.

He knew all that, and yet…

Sam forced himself to concentrate on what she was saying.

"I'm surprised that Aurora doesn't have the fattest police force in the country. Thank God everyone in the family's so into physical fitness and working out." She made a mental note to get to the gym herself the first chance she got. She would need to add some reps to her workout. "Otherwise, we could probably just roll over the perps and squash them instead of taking them in."

The visual made him laugh. "Save the county a lot of money in court costs," he theorized.

Riley realized she was close to the apartment complex. That was fast. How was it that trips back from their destination always seemed so much quicker than the original trip there? She could have sworn that they'd gotten here in the blink of an eye.

"Please don't say that around Andrew," she begged. "The man will use it as an excuse to insist that we all eat more."

"My lips are sealed," he said as Riley guided the car into a spot in guest parking.

"Oh God, I hope not."

Did that just come out of her mouth? How the hell did she let that happen? Riley chastised herself. When in doubt, offer a diversion. She'd learned that, oddly enough, from her father.

"Um, let me help you with Lisa," she volunteered,

then quickly got out of the car before Sam had an opportunity to say anything.

Riley had the rear passenger door open and unstrapped Lisa from her seat before he could reach his daughter. Sam stepped back, watching her.

Acutely aware of him, Riley had no idea what was going on in Wyatt's head. Maybe it was better that way.

Very gently, she removed the sleeping girl from her car seat and scooped Lisa up. "Just unlock your front door," she requested.

Sam saw no reason to argue, or insist that he could take care of Lisa himself. Especially when he had a strong feeling that Riley, as usual, would win the argument.

Leading the way, he took out his key. "Why is it that when we were in the academy, I never noticed this 'take charge' personality of yours?"

They were friends back then, but for one reason or another, nothing more.

"Maybe because you were always surrounded by all those eager female rookies who were vying for your attention," she speculated.

Sam put his key in the lock, turning it. The time spent in the academy was all a blur, as if someone else had lived it. "I don't recall any eager rookies," he told her innocently.

Right, like she'd believe that. "Alzheimer's doesn't usually set in this early," she commented.

He held the door open for her. Riley walked into the apartment first. Behind her, Sam flipped the light switch, illuminating the area.

"Thanks," she murmured, cutting through the living room.

Making a left, she headed toward the former guest room, now Lisa's bedroom. The room had, in the last few weeks, undergone a major transformation. That was thanks in large part to the various things she had picked up for the little girl. Not to be left out, Brenda had donated a few things, as well. The anonymous feeling the room had had was gone. This was now definitely a room that belonged to a little girl.

Placing Lisa on the bed, Riley debated getting the sleeping child out of her clothes and into her pajamas. The next moment, she abandoned the idea. One night spent in her clothes wasn't going to hurt. If she started to change her, Lisa might wake up. Judging from how tense Sam seemed, he wouldn't exactly welcome an all-nighter.

Taking Lisa's shoes off, Riley threw the bedcover over the small body and let the little girl sleep.

Sam stood in the room, watching her and feeling a little useless—but not enough to take over. "Aren't you going to get her into her pajamas?" he asked, curious.

Riley shook her head, backing away from the canopied bed. Nice touch, she thought, admiring the frills that outlined the canopy.

"Lisa might wake up. It's not worth the trouble," she assured him. About to leave the room, Riley noticed that rather than turn them off, he lowered the overhead lights until they were very dim.

"Lisa's afraid of the dark," he explained.

She could certainly relate to that, she thought as she slipped out of the room. He eased the door closed behind him.

"So was I for the longest time."

She didn't add that right after Sanchez's murder, her fears had revisited her and she'd gone back to sleeping with the lights on. She'd continued doing that until sometime last week. The need to have every corner illuminated had passed, disappearing as mysteriously as it had come.

"I wasn't allowed to be afraid," Sam told her simply.

Riley stopped just short of the front door to turn around and look at him. "Wasn't 'allowed'?" she repeated in disbelief. What did permission have to do with it?

He didn't think of his father often. Unpleasant memories were best held at bay. He supposed that suddenly becoming one himself on such short notice had roused a great many incidents from his own childhood. He was determined to do the opposite of whatever had been done to him.

"My father told me leaving the light on in my room once I was in bed was a waste of electricity. He maintained that there was nothing in the dark that wasn't there in the light."

Thank God she'd had an understanding mother. "How did that work for you?"

One corner of his mouth lifted. "I spent ten years sleeping with my baseball bat."

Amusement entered Riley's eyes as she visualized him as a small boy in bed with his Louisville Slugger.

"Until you found that girls had more curves?" she guessed whimsically.

"And were a lot softer," he added, playing along. In truth, it had taken him some time to get over his need to protect himself.

She was on dangerous ground and she knew it. Taking a breath, Riley told herself it was time to go home. She took a step toward the door, moving backward.

"Well, hope you had a good time," she told him. Was that as inane as it sounded?

"We did," he assured her. "Thanks for inviting us." And then he hesitated.

Part of him would regret this, he thought. The other part would regret it if he didn't at least try.

"You know, you don't have to go just yet. Would you like something to drink?" he suggested.

"Why Detective Wyatt, are you trying to get me to take in spirits?" she teased. "If I do, I won't be able to drive home for several hours."

His smile was warm. Disarming. She felt herself sinking. "Maybe that's part of the idea."

Breathe, damn it, Riley, breathe. "And what's the rest of the idea?"

His eyes slid over her. She could almost feel their caress. "I thought that maybe that could work itself out slowly."

Why did she suddenly feel as if she was standing on the edge of a precipice? One that was utterly unstable and threatened to give way beneath her feet at any second?

"No previews?" she questioned. "I always love seeing coming attractions when I go to the movies."

"Previews you want, previews you'll get," he murmured softly. So softly that she inclined her head toward him in order to hear.

That was exactly when her lips were suddenly captured.

Chapter 12

Riley knew she should pull away.

Sooner or later, most likely sooner, there would be hell to pay for this huge transgression, this blurring of lines that separated her professional life from her private one.

But she didn't care.

Logic and common sense didn't stand a ghost of a chance in the face of the heat generated by the mere touch of his lips on hers. The heat that she now found consuming her body.

Giving in to the pleasure, Riley wrapped her arms around Sam's neck. As she did so, she curved her body into his. The fact that he wanted her, really wanted her, registered instantly. And just as instantly, it created a yearning within her.

The kind of yearning that she hadn't experienced in a very long time.

Maybe never.

His hands, which had initially framed her face when he first kissed her, now moved away, sliding along her sides. Encircling her body. Holding her closer than a heartbeat.

And all the while he deepened the kiss, silently making this moment an event to celebrate.

Riley desperately tried to hold up her part, kissing him back for all she was worth. Not just absorbing sensations but creating them, as well. Her pride demanded it.

She got caught in her own trap.

Riley's head was spinning. Badly.

She wanted to attribute it to something common, like the lack of oxygen, but she knew better. Ever since she was a little girl, she could hold her breath an inordinate amount of time. This kiss went far beyond that.

Before she was fully conscious of her actions, she found that her fingers worked away at the buttons on Sam's shirt, pushing them out of their holes, tugging out the ends of the shirt and swiftly moving it away from his chest.

As she slid the material from his shoulders, Sam caught her hands in his and forced himself to draw his head back. To draw his lips away from hers.

His eyes searched her face for his answer even as he asked, "Riley, are you sure?"

He'd called her Riley, which he'd never done before. This was the private woman, not the detective, he was addressing. The private woman who was being seduced, who was melting. And the private woman was oh so sure she wanted this, *needed* this no matter what tomorrow would demand as payment for her involvement.

"I'm sure," Riley whispered, her breath feathering along his mouth, along his skin.

Something flared in his eyes. Desire? Oh, God, she hoped so.

"Then far be it from me to say no," he breathed, trying to sound as if he was teasing her.

"It better be far," Riley warned.

The truth be known, she was ready to explode right here, right now. And would have if he had pulled away. To stop just as everything within her had been primed to continue.

She hadn't realized just how much she wanted Sam until he'd kissed her. Now, she was fairly certain that the world would come to an abrupt, jarring end if he just stopped, even if he was trying to be chivalrous.

Riley splayed her hands over his chest. Hard muscles seemed to ripple beneath her palms. She could feel her excitement literally multiplying with each moment that passed.

"I had no idea you were so ripped," she murmured, her eyes on his.

"Lots of things you have no idea about," Sam told her, his voice rumbling low.

Exciting her.

He was right. There was a great deal she didn't know about this man. But she knew she placed her life in his hands every day, trusting him to have her back. Trusting him to be there for her.

How much more was there?

Trust was the most important ingredient in their relationship. In *every* relationship. The rest was minor in comparison.

Except that right now, it didn't feel so minor, these things he was causing to happen inside her. His lips skimmed the sensitive skin just beneath her chin, just along her throat. The fire in her veins increased, raising to astonishing heights she wasn't sure she could properly control.

His shirt stripped from his body, Sam began to return the favor. His lips pressed against hers, he undid the ends of her halter. The double knot stubbornly resisted, then finally came undone.

The two sides of the halter hung about her, tempting him. He could feel his breath catch in his throat.

His mouth curving against hers, he coaxed the material away from her body and discovered that, just as he'd suspected, Riley hadn't worn a bra beneath the virgin white top.

With patient movements, he kneaded her skin, bringing his palms in closer with each agonizingly slow pass until he finally cupped her breasts.

When he heard her breath catch, felt the swell of her breasts beneath his hands, Sam was certain something had ignited inside his soul.

God, he wanted her.

But if this was going to go any further, it couldn't be

here, out in the open in the living room. They were completely exposed here. If Lisa suddenly woke up and came in search of him, there was nowhere to hide.

Rather than launch into any explanations, he scooped a surprised Riley up into his arms and moved across the room, heading toward his bedroom.

Her heart pounded harder. "How did you know?" she breathed.

He hadn't a clue what she was referring to. Was she talking about their kiss? About the fact that they were about to make love? Or was it something else? Riley was *not* a woman he could read like a book. He needed a translation.

"Know what?" he asked as he shouldered his door open, then closed it again, this time using his back.

She laced her arms around his neck. "That I've always had this Rhett Butler fantasy," she whispered, "about being carried off to a bedroom."

Sam knew he should capitalize on this stroke of blind luck, play it up to his advantage. Most men, he knew, would have done just that. But he wasn't most men. Besides, lies had a way of backfiring and he wanted to take no chances.

"I didn't," he told her. "The moment just called for it."

And that, in part, was true. Because if he had remained out there a moment longer, things like protecting his daughter from too much age-inappropriate education would have plummeted to the bottom of his list of things to do in the heat of his desire.

That meant, Riley thought as another surge of excitement shot through her, that Sam was a natural. He was a romantic without even having to think about it. And that was excellent. Because the last thing she wanted either one of them to do right now was think. This wasn't the time for it, for detailed thoughts to wedge their way into what was happening.

All she wanted was to savor these sensations rushing through her. Savor the feel of his hands on her skin, his mouth on hers, doing wonderful, clever things and making her feel like a Roman candle about to go off at any second, illuminating the darkness.

She felt the mattress against her back as he laid her down, felt the impression of his body against hers as he sank to join her. And she felt her breath all but vanishing as his mouth began to work its way along her torso.

While his lips fueled the fire within her, she could feel his fingers working away at the snap on her shorts. The material parted as he slid the zipper down. Ever so slowly, Sam moved the material along her hips. The slower he moved, the more excited she felt, her flesh burning for the caress of his.

She raised her hips, allowing him to rid her of the last of her clothing as he tugged away both her shorts and white thong.

A frenzy assaulted her. Opening the snap on his jeans, she began to tug them off, trying to sweep them away with just a few well-placed movements.

Riley felt her heart pounding harder and harder as she struggled to divest him of the jeans while he all but held her captive with his magical mouth.

She could feel the eruption gathering, growing in volume and force.

Threatening to go off suddenly.

When Sam pressed the heel of his hand against her core, she climaxed for the first time. That had never happened to her before, not from the mere touch of a man's hand.

The very sensation stole her breath away.

Arching so that she could feel his hand pressing harder against her, the desire for more filled her entire being. Raising her head, she caught his lips, pressing hers against them. A heated passion assaulted her in waves.

Their bodies mingled as their limbs tangled with one another and Riley moved on top of him. Their mouths slanted over and over again, unable to be satiated.

Demanding more.

Damn but this was different, Sam thought. He'd expected her to be hot, expected to enjoy her while creating a web of pleasure for her, but this went beyond anything he'd imagined. The intensity throbbing through his veins was something he'd never experienced before.

He could feel his pulse racing, his hunger increasing at a breathtaking rate, overpowering him and making it very, very difficult for him to hold himself in check as long as he had planned.

There were no plans anymore, no blueprints on how to proceed. They were caught up in the fire and had burned up.

He was being swept away by a woman he had seriously

underestimated. He had thought that making love with Riley would be a pleasant, pleasurable experience. This went so far beyond that that it couldn't even be measured.

He wanted to reach that final moment, to crest and feel the last, breathtaking surge sweeping through his body. And yet, he still wanted to hold onto the promise of all that was to come, to extend this experience for as long as he could.

This wasn't normal.

This wasn't like him.

What the hell was she doing to him?

Still struggling for control, Sam flipped so that he got Riley onto her back again. He saw the surprise in her eyes, the signs of mounting anticipation vibrating throughout her being. Pleased, he began to work his way down her slick, supple body. Nipping at the tempting curves, gliding his tongue along her heated flesh. Priming her with his warm breath that skimmed against her skin.

He heard Riley moan as his mouth teased the center of her passion.

Empowered, imprisoned, he began to use his tongue to flirt with, then press against, her moist, heaving and more-than-willing flesh.

Oh, God, she couldn't catch her breath. Sam had stolen it from her.

Feeling as if she was in the midst of an out-of-body experience, Riley raised her hips up higher, offering herself to him. Grasping a slice of paradise as the explosion racked her body. She didn't care about equality, about doing to him what he was doing to her. She just wanted this to go on and on.

And for a moment, it did.

Time seemed to stand still as the sensation swelled and continued.

And then she fell back, exhausted and spent beyond words. Or so she thought.

The next moment, Sam began to move his heated body along hers. Tantalizing her.

Her heart was already pounding hard enough to break through her rib cage. But when she felt him enter her, it sped up even more, beating double-time. The confinements of exhaustion fell away from her.

Riley wrapped her legs around his torso, the rhythm of her body echoing his as the pace heightened. Their movement became increasingly more frantic. She felt Sam wrap his arms about her, holding her to him as if he intended to absorb her wholly into himself.

That excited her. Everything *about* this man and the magic he wove excited her.

She held on tightly, desperate to keep pace, wanting to feel exactly what he felt at the final moment of impact.

And then it happened.

She reached the peak of the summit with him, felt the fireworks showering around her and prayed that somehow, it could go on forever. And even though it didn't, even though she could feel the euphoria recede, the sense of contentment that overshadowed the wonder remained with her for far longer than she'd anticipated.

Gladdening her heart.

As she caught her breath, Riley went on holding him to her. Went on savoring everything about the coupling that had taken her by such storm. Slowly, ever so slowly, her breathing evened out.

This had to be what a person felt like when they were struck by lightning, Sam thought, his body still tingling all over. He struggled to get some kind of a grip on himself.

He succeeded only moderately.

Afraid of crushing Riley, he slowly slid off, moving to her side. He was surprised when she turned her body into his. Surprised and pleased more than words could possibly express.

He smiled into her eyes as he closed his arms around her and held her to him.

"You're full of surprises, McIntyre," he said, whispering the words against her hair.

McIntyre.

Not "Riley" but "McIntyre." Was he trying to distance himself from what had just happened? Now that they had made love, did he want to reestablish the boundaries of their ongoing relationship? Did this make her sad, or provide her with the safety net she so badly needed?

Damn, but nothing made sense right now. She couldn't think, couldn't see her way clearly to any one sentiment yet.

"I like keeping you on your toes," she finally answered. She felt him laugh and the sound rumbled against her chest. She turned her head to look at him. "What?"

Amusement curved the corners of his mouth. "Let's just say it wasn't my toes that were being called into action."

She could almost feel his smile against her hair, against her forehead. "Sorry, anatomy wasn't my best subject in school."

He trailed his fingertips along her curves, stroking her ever so slowly. Excitement began to vibrate between them. "I would have never guessed. You seemed pretty knowledgeable to me."

"Smoke and mirrors," she quipped, though it was beginning to take considerable effort to remain focused on what he was saying.

"Felt a little more solid than smoke to me," he told her.

She raised her head to look at him. She'd always disliked women who insisted on having a relationship mapped out for them at every conceivable turn. But Sam *was* her partner and she was pretty sure that they had just violated at least several very basic ground rules.

"Is what just happened going to get in our way?" she asked.

He was quiet for a moment, as if considering what she'd just asked from all possible angles. "Well, that depends."

Her eyes never left his face. She'd looked at him countless times. So why did she suddenly feel this on-rush of heat, of excitement? How had the dynamics between them changed so much?

"On?" she asked.

Sam ran the back of his hand along her cheek. Wanting her. "On whether or not we stop to do this when we're supposed to be going after the bad guy."

"Seriously," Riley pressed.

Humor played along his mouth. "What makes you think I wasn't being serious?" Pulling her to him so that her body was suddenly on top of his, Sam stroked the sides of her torso. Watching in fascination as he saw desire flaring in her eyes. "I was deadly serious," he told her, raising his head to capture her lips again.

Instantly undone, she didn't press the subject again for a good long while. It amazed her that she could be so hungry so fast after feasting for so long.

But she was.

Chapter 13

It didn't take long.

Another home invasion occurred Wednesday, four days later. The invasion had all the earmarks of the other three cases. The thieves entered the house without having to resort to force despite the fact that, according to the frightened homeowners, every single window in the house was closed and locked, as were the front and back doors.

The inhabitants, this time a couple in their early seventies, had been in bed, asleep, like all the other victims. They'd been rousted, dragged from their bed, tied up and then chloroformed while their home was ransacked.

"There's got to be a common element here, there has to be. What is it that we're missing?" Riley demanded for the umpteenth time, pacing in front of the bulletin board where they had religiously tacked up all the available information on each invasion.

"A lot of sleep," Sam murmured. He sat at his desk, his chair turned around so that he faced the bulletin board. Nothing seemed to stand out to him either.

The tone of his voice wedged itself into her admittedly scattered thoughts. Riley turned looked at her partner.

Afraid that Saturday night would change things between them, she could have saved herself the trouble of worrying. The following Monday, when she came into work, Sam had behaved as if it was business as usual, making absolutely no mention of what had transpired between them. Taking her partner's cue, relieved and yet not so relieved, Riley had done the same. And continued to do so.

But occasionally, she'd catch Sam watching her, an unreadable expression on his face.

Or maybe that was just wishful thinking on her part—or her pride. After all, what woman wanted to believe that she was forgettable or could be so easily dismissed?

She hadn't exactly expected Sam to sweep her into his arms when she walked into the squad room, but a random private word or two, a secret, intimate glance, wouldn't have been entirely out of order. After all, she was fairly certain that the sheets on his bed had gotten really scorched Saturday night before she, exhausted, had elected to go home rather than come up with an excuse for Lisa in the morning as to why she was still there in the clothes she'd worn the day before.

"You losing sleep over this, Wyatt?" Riley asked archly.

"This among other things," he answered. And then he lowered his voice before continuing. "Lisa wants to know when you're coming over."

"Lisa," she repeated.

Was he being straightforward and just relaying his daughter's question, or was he using his daughter as a shill to cover up the fact that *he* wanted to know when she was coming over?

God, when did things suddenly become this complicated?

"Yeah, Lisa." His expression continued to be unreadable. "You remember, short little thing." He held his hand up approximately three and a half feet from the floor. "Talks like an old person even though she's only six." He paused, as if debating whether or not to say the next thing. "She wants to know if I did something to make you stop coming over. I told her I didn't think so, but she's not convinced." His eyes held hers, pregnant with things that weren't being said. "Did I?"

"No." She cleared her throat, wondering where this sudden case of nerves came from. Nerves neatly wrapped around a ray of sunshine. "Then I guess I'll have to come over." This time, she was the one looking into his eyes. "If Lisa wants to see me."

He glanced away, back at the bulletin board. Sam tilted his chair. "Yeah, she does."

"If you two are finished talking about your social agenda," Barker bit off, suddenly materializing behind them, "maybe one of you can tell me how the investigation's coming along?"

The lieutenant's dark brown eyes shifted from Sam to her.

That proved it, Riley thought. The man was the devil. "Which one?" she asked him politely.

"All of them," he growled.

Sam rose from his chair, moving so that his body was between Barker and Riley.

"The Hayworths kept to themselves for the most part," Sam told the lieutenant. "According to the descriptions they gave the first officer on the scene and then again to us, the two robbers were the same ones who robbed the other three houses. As far as McIntyre and I can see, this new couple has almost nothing in common with the other victims." Before Barker could comment, Sam enumerated. "They all drive different cars, have different careers—the Hayworths are retired," he inserted. "Move in different circles."

Barker was in no mood to play review. "Yeah, yeah, I've heard it all before and I don't want to hear it again," he snapped. "I also don't want to hear any more excuses. The next thing I want to hear is that you've cracked the case." His eyes swept over Sam and Riley, then took in the two detectives sitting closest to them, Sung and Allen. His manner was clear. As far as he was concerned, the whole department was responsible for this less-than-stellar performance. "Do I make myself clear?"

"Absolutely," Riley replied with the kind of cheerful enthusiasm she knew annoyed Barker and got under the man's skin.

The lieutenant's dark brown eyes grew even darker

as he narrowed them to focus only on her. "As long as we understand each other."

With that, the former marine turned on his well-worn heel and stalked back into his glass office. The blinds remained opened so that nothing would escape his attention.

"He makes Darth Vader come off like Pollyanna," Riley commented, keeping her voice low even though Barker had closed his door. She'd turned her back to the man's office. Barker was ornery enough to have learned how to read lips. "By the way, you didn't have to run interference for me," she told Sam. "I can take care of myself."

"Haven't the slightest idea what you're talking about, McIntyre," Sam said, his expression giving nothing away. He took his jacket off the back of his chair and threw it on. "C'mon, let's see if we can get the Hayworths to remember what they did in the last forty-eight hours." He saw the puzzled expression on her face and explained. "Maybe we'll get lucky and that'll give us the clue we need to solve this damn thing."

"I had no idea you were an optimist," she commented, grabbing her purse. She hurried after him.

Sam considered her remark as they walked out. "Must be the company I keep," he decided.

Riley smiled in response.

They tracked Professor Cahil to his office at the college.

"You again?" the professor groaned as he looked up to see who was coming into his office. Biting off an oath, Cahil set aside the less-than-engrossing term paper he was reading. "Aren't you people out of questions yet?" he asked, exasperated.

"Just a few more, Professor. It'll be painless and we'll be out of your hair before you know it," Riley promised.

The professor seemed less than convinced. "Not soon enough to suit me," he assured the two detectives. "Well, sit down." He gestured to the two chairs before his desk. "We might as well get this over with."

Sam waited for Riley to take a seat before he sat down in his. "Can you tell us what you did the two days before the robbers came into your house?"

Suspicion narrowed the professor's gaze. "Why?" he challenged.

This time Riley ran interference. "We're trying to see if you and the other victims might have all done the same thing."

Cahil had an air about him that said he didn't consider himself to be like anyone else. That would have been too common. "Like what?"

"That's just it," Sam interjected. "We don't know."

Contempt flared in the professor's expression. "There isn't a hell of a whole lot you people do know, is there?"

"We know uncooperative people when we talk to them," Riley said simply. She moved forward in her chair. "Now, you don't like being a victim, we get it. And I'm sorry if we're bothering you, Professor, but we're doing our best to recover your property. But to make any headway, we need your help. Yours and the other people who were robbed.

"We're working under the assumption that there's

some common thread, something that you all did, that pulls this together." Her tone was polite, but firm as she said, "Now if you could please just go over the two days before the robbery in as much detail as possible, we would greatly appreciate it." She looked at Cahil, waiting.

"Very well."

Sighing, the professor closed his eyes. To the best of his ability, he began to summon back the two days in question.

"You're pretty persuasive when you want to be," Sam commented as they left the professor's office less than twenty minutes later and walked through the visitor parking lot just beyond the criminology department's three-story building.

Riley grinned. "As the next to the youngest of four, I found being persuasive rather essential to my survival." She waited for Sam to unlock the doors, then got into the car. "Two down, two more to go."

"Can't say I'm feeling too hopeful," he admitted, putting the key into the ignition and turning it. The car started. "So far, beyond the essentials of eating and doing a few basic things involved with getting ready to face the day, the professor's two days don't sound as if they have anything in common with the Hayworths' two days."

"Keep the faith, Wyatt," she urged as they backtracked their way off the campus. "The day is still young."

He blew out a breath as he just missed a light that would have allowed him to get onto the main thorough-

fare. Where was all this impatience coming from?
"Yeah, but I feel like I'm getting older by the minute."

She smiled at him. "You'll feel young again once we
make a breakthrough."

But they didn't and consequently, he didn't.

The case began to wear on Sam. Riley was right, they
were missing something in plain sight and it frustrated
the hell out of him.

Once they were finished taking information from
the Marstons and the Wilsons, it was time to clock out
for the day.

True to her word, Riley followed him to Brenda's
house where they picked up Lisa. The little girl was
nothing short of overjoyed when she saw Riley. The
second she did, Lisa ran up to her and, standing on her
toes, she wrapped her small arms around Riley. Lisa
held on tightly and had to be coaxed to let go, which she
did only after Riley promised to come over.

A warm feeling spread through Riley as she caught
a glimpse of the three of them in Brenda's hall mirror
when they were leaving the house.

They looked like a real family, she thought.

She'd never thought of herself in those terms
before. Never really thought about being a wife *or* a
mother. But now, there it suddenly was, front and
center. And the idea had a charm and a pull that was
very difficult to ignore.

Too bad, Riley thought as she adjusted the straps on
Lisa's car seat, that it was never going to happen.

* * *

A pattern began to form. A pattern Riley knew she could easily get accustomed to and one that she was equally aware that she *shouldn't* allow.

It was happening anyway.

By day, she and Wyatt were professional partners, working feverishly to handle all the cases they caught while still seeking that one breakthrough. They needed to solve what had become a major obsession with the news media: the home invasion robberies.

And then, most nights, they were lovers, burning away the edges of the night until it was time for her to finally go back to her house.

Every time she did, she would find Howard waiting up for her like a doting grandfather, an indulgent, knowing expression on his face.

"So how's it going?" the retired engineer asked after another three weeks had passed.

"The case?" she responded.

He waved his hand at that. "I know you can't talk about an ongoing case—Egan taught me that," his voice swelling with pride the way it always did whenever he mentioned his late son. "And everything else I want to know about them is plastered all over the news anytime I want to catch up. No, I'm asking how's it going with you and that young man you've been keeping company with?"

Keeping company with. What a lovely, old-fashioned term for what she and Wyatt did together. Four weeks since the first time and the lovemaking was only getting better. Hotter. If it became any more so, she would need the fire department on standby.

"What makes you think I'm 'keeping company' with anyone?"

"You've got the same glow my Katie did when we were," and here he cleared his throat, whether because he needed to or by design wasn't evident, "keeping company. Is it that partner of yours?" he asked, then smiled. "It is, isn't it? Nice-looking boy," he said with a nod. "Hair's a little long for my taste, but he seems all right otherwise. He treating you well?" Howard asked.

"Howard, I think you've just exceeded your allotment of questions."

"Because if he isn't," Howard continued as she walked up her driveway toward her front door, "you just send him on to me and I'll set him straight."

It was hard not to laugh, given that the man had the body of a large Halloween skeleton, but she wouldn't have hurt Howard's feelings for the world. "Good night, Howard," she called out.

"Good night, Riley. Sleep tight."

Sleep fast, she corrected silently, because there weren't all that many hours left until daylight and her shift arrived.

But as well intentioned as Howard's concern was, it stirred up some questions that hovered in the back of her mind, questions she would have rather put off. Questions she knew she had to face eventually.

This "thing" with her and Wyatt wasn't a fling anymore, or just a flirtation that had temporarily deepened and she knew it. It had become so much more. She was attached to Lisa and, what was worse, she realized she was falling in love with Wyatt.

What falling? she silently jeered as she got ready for work the following day. She'd already fallen for the man, hook, line and sinker. For better or for worse, she was there, treading through No Man's Land, most likely alone because even as she felt the words "I love you" bubbling up in her throat, threatening to come spilling out of her mouth, she was almost certain those same words would not be echoed back to her.

Except maybe out of a sense of guilt.

No, Wyatt wasn't the type to do anything because he felt guilty. There wasn't even a token "I love you" in her future and she knew it.

Riley sighed. She needed to put a stop to this romance, to back away before she couldn't. But even as she gave herself the pep talk, she knew it would be more than difficult to end things between them. Still, she knew she had to make a concerted effort.

So much easier said than done.

Even as she tried, she found herself blocked at every turn. Each time she wanted to offer an excuse, to say no, that she couldn't go with him to pick up Lisa, the words never emerged.

Instead, she said, "Sure," and went along, basking in the bright light she saw in Lisa's eyes every time the little girl saw her.

After that, staying for dinner was a given. Besides,

there were cooking lessons involved. She wasn't even sure how it started, but somehow she gave Lisa simple cooking lessons and the two of them would prepare dinner together.

That had to stop, too.

Soon.

This time, on the trip home, Lisa was fairly bursting with news, but she kept it in until they walked into the apartment.

"Tonight," Lisa declared the moment the door was closed, "you don't have to cook, Riley. We're having pizza. My treat," she declared proudly, beaming.

"How is this going to be your treat?" Riley asked, looking toward Wyatt. But he indicated that his lips were sealed.

"I get an allowance," Lisa informed her with a little toss of her head. "Daddy gives me money and I saved it up, so this is my treat," she repeated, her eyes dancing with glee.

Riley exchanged looks with Sam. Lisa had just called him Daddy. Not Sam, but Daddy. Was this the first time? One glance at the surprised expression on his face gave her the answer. She had intended to begin the weaning process tonight, begging off from dinner and then, within a few days, from the ritual of picking Lisa up at Brenda's. But how could she say no after this? Lisa had just called Wyatt something other than his given name and offered to pay for the dinner with her own money. Turning the little girl down would be heartbreaking. For both of them.

So she said yes and she stayed.

But Riley promised herself that the moment the little girl was tucked into bed, she was going home. Tonight, there would be no lovemaking, no getting lost in Sam's arms. Tonight was going to be the beginning of the rest of her life. Without Sam.

Much as she didn't want to, Riley knew she had to take a stand somewhere. And this was somewhere.

Bedtime came all too quickly. She followed the ritual, getting Lisa ready for bed, then reading to her. She'd stumbled a few times. The lump in her throat kept getting in the way. But finally, Lisa drifted off to sleep.

The moment she did, Riley crept out of Lisa's room. She made her way to the living room. Expecting to see Sam, she was relieved when she didn't. Grabbing her purse, she quickly made her way to the front door.

"Where are you going?"

She froze when she heard his voice behind her. Without turning around, she answered, "I've got to go home."

Walking around to face her, Sam took the purse from her hand. That smile that always burrowed into the pit of her stomach, creating a squadron of butterflies, was on his lips. "No, you don't."

Telling herself to be strong, Riley reclaimed her purse, pulling it out of his hand. "Yes, I do," she insisted.

The teasing expression on his face faded. Concern entered his eyes as he searched her face. "Something wrong?"

"No. Yes." Damn, why did he always make her feel so tongue-tied? No one else ever did.

A hint of steely amusement curved his lips. "I didn't realize I asked a multiple-choice question."

"You didn't." Sighing, she tried again. "Look, this has been great—"

Has been. As in the past. Something *was* wrong. Sam braced himself. "But?"

Taking another breath didn't help. The ache she felt kept growing. "But it has to stop."

He wanted to grab hold of her shoulders and shake some sense into her head. It took extreme restraint just to stand there and ask, "Why?"

Such a simple word, so fraught with intense repercussions. "Because it's not going anywhere."

Was she pressing him for a commitment? Or trying to find a way out? Or was she just testing him? "Why does it have to 'go' somewhere? Why can't it just be?" he asked. "Sometimes things just have to remain the way they are in order to go forward later."

"Later" was a vague word that kept company with "never." This had to stop now, before the disappointment got too big for her to handle.

"Maybe," she allowed, letting him think she might agree with him. "But right now, I need to sort things out, think them through."

He would never force her to do anything she didn't want to do, be anywhere she didn't want to be. But letting her walk away, even for an evening, wasn't easy. "All right," he finally said. "If that's what you want."

No, that wasn't what she wanted. She wanted him. And Lisa. She knew that wasn't going to happen, not in the way she needed it to. Squaring her shoulders, she murmured, "I'll see you tomorrow."

As she put her hand on the doorknob, he asked, "No goodbye kiss?"

She looked at him over her shoulder, still holding onto the doorknob, as if that could somehow ground her. "If I kiss you goodbye, I won't leave."

"Sure you will." Sam turned her around and drew her into his arms. "You're stronger than that."

But she wasn't.

Chapter 14

Sam Wyatt was a dirty fighter. There was no other way to view what had happened but that, Riley thought several hours later when she finally got into her car and drove home. Once Wyatt kissed her, it was all over.

She and Sam made love. But even though every fiber of her being wanted to remain, locked tightly in his arms, she forced herself to leave after only a heavenly two hours had gone by. The earliest she'd left his apartment since they had begun sleeping together—or not sleeping together as the case was.

She should have been stronger than that, Riley upbraided herself. She *used* to be stronger than that. What was wrong with her?

Tomorrow, Riley solemnly swore. Tomorrow she

was going to be stronger. Tomorrow she'd leave right after Lisa went to bed, no wavering, no second thoughts, no side glances at Wyatt that only undermined her resolve. She'd make Wyatt read the bedtime story to his daughter instead of her and then slip out while he was busy.

It sounded like a plan.

Well, she tried to console herself, at least Howard would get to bed earlier tonight. Howard. Funny how her eccentric neighbor had taken her under his wing like that, appointing himself her guardian angel. Lately it seemed like most of their exchanges took place just before she walked into her house.

She would invite him next time the chief held another party at his place. With work—and Sam—taking up so much of her time, she'd gotten out of the habit of extending invitations to the older man. She needed to remedy that, remembering how difficult it had been the first time around. Riley turned off the main drag and into her development. For the most part, despite his apparent adoption of her, the retired engineer liked to keep to himself. In the three years she'd lived next door to him, she'd only seen one visitor enter the house and that had been his other son, Ethan, visiting from back east.

As she approached Howard's house, she saw that, as usual, he'd left his porch light on. Riley smiled. A beacon on the runway to guide her home, she mused.

She began to slow down to almost a crawl, giving Howard a chance to get up from the window seat where he had kept vigil lately and open the front door.

But the front door didn't move.

Odd. Howard never failed to come out, even that time he was fighting a cold. It was as if all the pieces of his world weren't in place until he bid her good-night and saw her go into her own place.

Pulling up into her driveway, Riley turned off her ignition and waited a moment before getting out. There was still no movement at the other house.

Maybe Howard had finally decided she was a big girl, Riley thought with a smile. Or gotten what his son had called his obsessive-compulsive disorder under control. Whatever the reason, it didn't look as if she'd be saying good-night to him tonight.

Key in hand, Riley was about to insert it into her door when she sighed, pocketed the key and doubled back down the front path. Moving around the plum tree that separated their two properties, she walked up to Howard's porch.

Something wasn't right, she could feel it. Howard wouldn't just leave the porch light on and go to bed. It wasn't like him. Though leaving an outside light on was considered a deterrent against amateur burglars, she knew that Howard stubbornly considered it a flagrant waste of electricity and money.

When ringing the doorbell twice got no response, Riley knocked on the man's door. Hard. Head cocked, she listened intently for the familiar shuffling sound that meant he was approaching.

Nothing.

"Howard?" she called out, knocking again. Her uneasiness growing, Riley tried the doorknob. It gave under her hand.

Howard *never* left his door unlocked.

Training had Riley pulling out her service weapon and taking off the safety.

"Howard?" she called again, slowly pushing open the door. Light not just from the porch but from the city street light that was situated directly behind Howard's mailbox illuminated the dark living room. It took her a moment to focus.

Riley's heart slammed into her chest the second she saw the slumped figure on the floor. Howard was tied to a dining room chair and the chair was over on its side. Howard's mouth, arms and legs were bound tightly with duct tape.

The home invaders had been here, right here, on her home territory!

Riley felt sick to the bottom of her stomach and incredibly violated.

Her first impulse was to untie Howard, to remain with him and assure herself that he was all right. But the cop in her knew that she needed to clear the area first because if the robbers were still here, it could go badly for her, not to mention Howard.

They didn't kill their victims, she silently insisted, trying to comfort herself as she began to sweep through the rooms. Moving as quickly as she could and exercising just the barest minimum of caution, Riley swiftly swept through the rooms as best she could. It was harder than she'd expected.

Howard had done some really heavy-duty collecting since he'd last had her over, she noted. Books of all kinds, magazines, record albums were piled from floor to ceiling in several of the rooms, challenging anyone to get through or even access certain areas. The man was a serious pack rat—and she prayed that he would be able to spend a great many more years feeding his compulsion.

Done, Riley hurried back to her neighbor, pausing only in the kitchen to get a pair of scissors out of his utility drawer.

That, too, proved to be a challenge. All sorts of things were jammed into the drawer, as well as all the other drawers. Howard had never come across anything he wanted to throw out.

Finally finding the scissors, Riley rushed back into the living room. Dropping to her knees, she carefully began to cut apart the duct tape wound around him as tightly as a cocoon.

She was only halfway through when Howard groaned, sounding like a man struggling to wake up from a bad dream. There was the distinct odor of chloroform about him.

The irony of the situation was appalling to Riley. There she and Wyatt were, methodically trying to track down the home invaders and meanwhile, the larcenous duo had struck right under her nose. The worse part of it was that it had happened while she and Wyatt were busy making love.

But if she'd come home earlier, the invaders might not have struck yet and she'd have gone to bed, she realized. She wouldn't have known anything was wrong until the following night. She hardly even saw Howard before she left in the morning.

Something about the scenario didn't feel right, but she wasn't sure what it was.

Removing the last of the tape, she sat back on her heels, waiting for Howard to come around. His breathing was normal, and when she pressed her fingers to his throat, she found that his heart rate was only slightly elevated. At least the bastards hadn't given him a heart attack.

She placed a call to the firehouse located three miles from her development. After identifying herself and giving her shield number, she asked the person on the other end of the line to send a couple of paramedics over. She wanted them to check out Howard just in case.

And then she called Wyatt.

"You're sure they were the same ones?" Sam asked half an hour later. He'd just left Lisa, along with his apologies, at Brenda and Dax's house. The couple had assured him that there was nothing to apologize for, they understood the erratic life police detectives were forced to lead. Now that he was here, Sam could hardly believe what Riley was telling him.

The paramedics had arrived five minutes after she'd placed her call to them and, despite Howard's protests, had checked out the man from top to bottom. Except for the bump on his head, sustained when the chair was knocked over, the only thing that was wounded was Howard's pride.

"I should have been able to fight them off," he complained to Riley as the paramedics withdrew. "I placed second in my weight class at the gym."

Riley had heard the story more than once. "No disrespect intended, Howard," she said softly, gently rubbing her hand along his back, trying to soothe away his agitation, "but you did tell me that was almost fifty years ago."

And then it suddenly hit her. Riley realized what had been bothering her since she'd come on the scene to find him unconscious and bound to the chair. "Wait a minute, were you in bed?"

"No." He tried to rise to his feet from the sofa but his legs were a little wobbly. He sank back down again just as Wyatt and Riley reached out to catch him. "I was waiting up for you. Like always."

Wyatt looked to Riley for elaboration.

"Howard likes to make sure I get home in one piece," she told him. "He's my self-appointed guardian angel. Long story," she added before turning her attention back to her neighbor. "But if you weren't in bed—why would they have come in? They *always* come in when their victims are in bed."

"Did you have the lights on in the house?" Sam asked the man.

"No, why waste it?" Howard asked defensively. "It's not like I'm reading."

It still didn't make any sense to Riley. "But they would have seen you—and you would have seen them if you were by the window."

His cheeks turned a slight shade of pink. "I had to go to the bathroom," Howard mumbled. "They jumped me right when I came out," he accused, then shook his head. "I dunno who was more surprised, them or me. It looked like they were on their way to the staircase when I opened the bathroom door. Next thing I knew, the tall one was grabbing my arms, pinning them behind my back and the little guy started punching me. Dunno what *they* were afraid of since I couldn't use my hands."

She winced as she envisioned the scene. She could almost feel the blows, but this wasn't the time to be emotional. She had to be a detective first, not Howard's friend. This could be the break they'd been looking for. "Howard, this is very important, did you recognize either of them?"

"How could I?" he protested. "They were dressed in black with ski masks on."

She shook her head. "No, I mean was there something familiar about the way they moved, the way they talked? Was there anything unique to set them apart in your mind? A smell, perhaps. Did either of them call the other by a name?"

At each suggestion, Howard shook his head. Until she mentioned smell. "The little guy smelled like garlic," he told her. "And …"

That was what one of the other couples had said, she thought, suddenly excited. "And?" she coaxed.

"The tall, skinny one kept dropping his Gs. He sounded a little like that valet."

Sam and Riley exchanged glances. "What valet?" Sam asked.

"That one at that place—" Howard looked frustrated as he tried to summon the right words.

"Which one at what place, Howard?" Riley pressed gently.

Howard closed his eyes for a moment, regrouping.

All around them were members of the crime scene investigation unit, methodically going about their business, trying to piece together physical evidence. Riley heard one of the men complaining to the woman in charge that he'd almost gotten attacked by a tall stack of books. The stack, one of dozens, that had dislodged when he'd opened the door leading into the room.

"Ethan was here last week," Howard told her.

"I remember."

"Ethan?" Sam looked from Howard to her. "Who's Ethan?"

"His son," Riley said, not taking her eyes off Howard. "Go on."

"Ethan's a doctor," Howard tagged on. "He insisted on taking me to this fancy restaurant." He snorted his disapproval. "I used to get weekly paychecks that were smaller than what these people charged for a meal, but Ethan insisted we go there, said he was paying. So I said I'd drive."

That meant that they had driven to the restaurant in Howard's secondhand Mercedes. He babied that car, kept it in prime condition. Sundays would find him polishing and waxing the vehicle until it was almost blinding to look at.

Alarms went off in Riley's head.

One slanted glance toward Wyatt told her they were having a mutual epiphany.

"And you left your keys with the valet," Wyatt said out loud.

Obviously confused, Howard looked from Riley to her partner. "How else was he going to park my car?"

"Is your house key on the same key chain as your car key?" Riley asked him, doing her best not to raise her voice or allow the building excitement she felt to surface.

Again, Howard seemed puzzled. "I've only got the two keys," he told her. "Why should I keep them on separate key chains? It's easier to lose one of them that way," he pointed out.

Everything fell into place.

Oh, God, could it really be as simple as that? The valets had access to the keys and to the client's address because registrations were required to be kept in the glove compartment of each car on the road. All the valet needed to do was to copy down the address and make an impression of the house key. When his shift was over, he could take the impression to a locksmith who might be bribed to look the other way and have made a key.

Or who knows, maybe the valet could make the keys himself, Riley speculated. Once the valet made a copy of the key, he and his partner could drive to the address, case out the house and its surrounding neighborhood with a minimum of danger to see if a break-in would be profitable.

Wyatt knew what Riley was thinking. But he had a basic problem with the theory. "If the thieves have a copy of the key, why wouldn't they just break into the house during the day when everyone's gone?"

It was the simplest way to go, but simple didn't always mean best. "Because there's always a chance that someone might be in the house," she guessed. "Doing it at night fairly assures them that everyone's asleep so they can get the upper hand. Besides, I don't think it's just about the robbery."

"Then what?" Wyatt wanted to know.

"I think it's a power trip. The people they rob have things, can afford to go to fancy restaurants, are most likely better off than our thieves. To them, it's 'anything you've got, I can take away,' that sort of thing."

Riley turned to look at her neighbor. Saying her theory out loud had gelled it for her. She threw her arms around him and hugged Howard as gently as she could, trying not to let her enthusiasm get the better of her.

"Oh, Howard, I think you just might have solved the crime for us."

Howard looked almost bashful. "Glad I wasn't banged around for nothing," he mumbled.

Riley laughed and pressed a kiss to the large bare expanse just above his forehead.

"I'm just glad you're all right. I'll be right back," she promised, getting up. Moving to the far end of the living room, she took out her cell phone.

Wyatt followed her. "Who are you calling?"

About to press a number on the cell's keypad, she stopped for a second. "I'm going to see if our other victims ever went to The Crown Jewels Restaurant."

He glanced at his watch. It was now close to eleven o'clock. "Isn't it a little late to be calling?" he pointed out.

"Justice never sleeps." Riley pressed a single button and the phone on the other end of the line began to ring.

"You've got them on speed dial?" he asked.

"Sure. Just until the cases are solved. Why, don't you?" she asked.

But before Wyatt could answer, she held up her finger, asking for silence. She heard someone come on the line.

"Four out of five is a pretty good track record," Riley declared some twenty minutes later. She, Wyatt and Howard had adjourned to the kitchen to keep out of the crime scene investigators' way as she made the rest of her calls. "Everyone but the Marstons remember going to The Crown Jewels Restaurant some time before they were robbed."

"I'm sure they enjoyed going down memory lane with you at almost midnight," Sam commented.

"I doubt if any of them are heavy sleepers anymore," she answered. "And maybe they'll sleep better once we get the bad guys."

"But *are* they the bad guys if the Marstons never went to The Crown Jewels?" Sam asked. "Their home invasion was exactly like the others and we'd need a hundred percent match in order to establish—" Sam didn't get a chance to finish.

Riley's cell phone rang.

Flipping it open again, she put it against her ear. "McIntyre. Yes. What? Oh. Okay." Sam saw a radiant smile blooming on her lips. "Well, thank you for calling back, Mr. Marston. Yes, yes, that was extremely helpful. And yes, I would ground him if I were you. Uh-huh. I promise I'll let you know the second we find out. Goodbye."

"What's extremely helpful and who are you grounding?" Sam asked the second she flipped the cell phone closed again.

"You look like the cat that ate the canary," Howard observed, curiosity getting the better of him, as well.

Excitement vibrated in Riley's voice as she filled in Sam and Howard about the home invaders' other victim. "Mr. and Mrs. Marston didn't go to The Crown Jewels Restaurant, but it seems that their son took his dad's credit card and his girl there. Junior overheard the conversation and just confessed."

Howard shook his head. "Teenagers. Absolutely no respect for money these days."

"Not to mention that if he hadn't taken his girl there, his parents wouldn't have been targeted by the home invaders. He's probably going to be grounded until he collects social security," she commented just before clapping her hands together. "Okay, now we're batting a thousand. What do you say you and I have a late lunch at The Crown Jewels tomorrow? We'll use my car."

It seemed like the way to go. Except for one thing. "Why your car?" Sam asked.

"Elementary, my dear Watson. Your registration will tell them that you live in an apartment. These people only rob houses."

He conceded the point, but there was a larger one to consider. "This is a long shot, you know. There's no guarantee that they'll take the bait. I mean, they have to park hundreds of cars during the week."

"That's why I'm going to ask to borrow that rock that the chief gave Rose for their last anniversary. That, and a few other 'trinkets' from the family should do it. If I sparkle enough," she looked at Sam and batted her eyelashes, "I'm sure I'll move right up to the top of their list."

It crossed Sam's mind that Riley sparkled enough without any jewelry, but, since they weren't alone, he decided to keep that to himself.

Chapter 15

"I know you want to keep your neighbor out of this if possible, but I think we should bring those valets in for questioning. This plan of yours just isn't working," Sam told Riley.

He was sitting in his car, parked down the block and across the street from her house and talking to her via his cell phone. His muscles felt cramped and he was going just a little stir crazy.

As she sat in the dark in her living room, Riley hoped that the sight of her house locked down for the night would give the home invaders the go-ahead signal. So far, nothing had happened.

Though she didn't want to, she was beginning to agree with her partner. She and Wyatt had been at this for almost two straight weeks now with no success. Night after night went by and still no sign of the home invaders.

She'd thought for certain that flashing her borrowed jewelry would be a definite come-on to the robbers. That and the fact that when the valet had brought back her car, she'd loudly refused, as they'd previously agreed, to allow Wyatt to give the man a generous tip.

"You don't need to give him that big tip," she'd admonished. "For heaven's sake, it's not like he had to fight off some roving gang of bikers to bring the car to us. He just drove the thing around the corner. Honestly, Sam, you're just too generous for your own good."

If looks could kill, Riley would have been dead on the spot. The glare the valet had given her would have cut her to ribbons.

Maybe it had been the wrong valet. But he'd been tall and thin and looked exactly as Howard had described him. Besides, the valet dropped his Gs, just the way Howard had remembered.

Riley sighed into her phone. "You're probably right. This is getting us nowhere." For all she knew, they were still at square one, except she had a gut feeling that she was right: valets operating at The Crown Jewels Restaurant were behind the robberies. Nothing else made sense to her. "Go home to Lisa."

"Will do. Good night, partner," Sam said, flipping his phone closed.

He tossed the phone onto the seat next to him. The seat Riley ordinarily occupied. This surveillance cut into not just the time he spent with his daughter, but the time he spent with Riley, as well. They hadn't gotten together intimately since this surveillance began and he missed her. Missed being with her. Missed the scent of her skin, the feel of her body against his. He missed the sound of her breath growing erratic as they came together, pleasuring one another.

He'd never felt this way about a woman before, not to this extent and not for this long. He'd certainly never caught himself longing for a woman the way he longed for Riley.

This was all new to him and confusing as hell.

Or maybe not so confusing, just scary, he amended, because, like it or not, he felt vulnerable.

Sam glanced at his watch. He knew Riley was right, he should be getting home. For the last few days, Riley's mother had volunteered to stay with the little girl so that Lisa could sleep in her own bed and not have her routine constantly disrupted.

Six months ago if anyone would have told him that the Chief of Detectives' wife would be babysitting for his daughter and that he would be physically—and emotionally—involved with the chief's stepdaughter, he would have laughed until gasping for breath. He'd had no daughter and he just wasn't the lasting kind. Women came and went in his life like the seasons back east, one fading away just as another came along.

What a difference half a year made, he mused.

Maybe he'd wait just a little longer, Sam decided. He didn't want to leave too early, just in case…

Forty-five minutes later, tired, Sam called it a night.

There was no point in doing this, he thought. The robbers weren't coming. He needed to go before he was too exhausted to drive and fell asleep at the wheel.

Putting his key into the ignition, he turned it on. The car quietly came to life. Going up the next driveway, he turned his car around and began to drive down the street that eventually led out of the development.

It was late and hardly any vehicles were on the road. Anyone with an ounce of sense was home. Where he needed to be.

Even though it hardly felt like home without Riley there.

Don't start in, just get home, Sam silently lectured himself.

Coming to the edge of the development, he passed a car heading in. Sam pressed his lips together to stifle a yawn. Damn, but he was tired.

Riley bolted upright.

Was that a noise, or just an overly realistic dream spilling out into her awakened state?

She listened intently, trying to decide.

Leaving her living room, at the last minute she'd left a pile of books right by the front door—just in case. If someone came in, they'd knock the books over when they opened the door.

That was what she'd heard, the books being knocked over. She was sure of it.

Her heart pounding, Riley grabbed the telephone receiver to call for backup.

There was no dial tone.

The line was dead.

And she'd left her cell phone downstairs.

Thank God she hadn't put her service revolver away in its usual place, she thought. Instead, she'd brought it to her bedroom and placed it on the nightstand. She put her hand on it now for reassurance.

Slipping quickly out of bed, she made to the doorway as quietly as possible. Holding her breath, she crept to the hallway.

Someone from the left grabbed her by the waist, pulling her so hard, he all but knocked the air out of her. The gun was wrenched out of her hand.

And then there was this awful pain in the back of her head. He'd hit her with something hard.

Riley struggled to keep from fading into the darkness that grabbed her. Instead of fighting back, she pretended to be limp, hoping that the home invader would drop his guard.

Whoever had hit her was carrying her down the stairs. And then she felt herself being roughly deposited onto a chair. It was now or never. She knew what came next. Duct taping her to the chair. The second she made contact with the seat, she leaped up, grappling with her assailant.

She'd caught him off guard. But not his partner. Behind her Riley heard a gun being cocked.

"I wouldn't do that if I were you, bitch," a raspy voice warned.

"Good advice. I suggest you follow it."

A split second earlier, the unlocked door had slammed against the opposite wall. Riley whirled around and saw that Sam had his gun out and pointed toward the robber with the gun on her.

Some kind of inner instinct had her envisioning the next move. The shorter of the two men spun around, his gun still in hand, except that this time, the weapon was pointed toward Sam.

His eyes looked crazy enough for him to use it.

With a guttural scream, Riley launched herself at the man with the gun, grabbing his arm and trying to point it up in the air. The distinct odor of garlic assaulted her nose. The gun discharged, the bullet going wild and hitting the overhead chandelier just as the sound of sirens filled the air.

Backup, she thought, a tidal wave of relief washing over her. Sam had called for backup. God love 'im.

"I give up, man, I give up!" the taller of the two cried, raising his hands in the air. They were trembling. "I don't have a gun. The gun's Jason's. It's not mine."

"You don't have the guts to even hold a gun," the one called Jason retorted in disgust, taunting his partner. "You'd be nowhere without me."

"And now you'll be in jail because of him," Sam chimed in sarcastically.

Quickly stuffing Jason's weapon into his belt, he handcuffed the man and turned toward Riley. He was about to ask her where her handcuffs were when he saw her pallor.

Pointing his gun at both the men, he glanced at her again, concerned. "Are you all right?"

"Just fine," she answered before she sank to her knees and everything went black.

Her eyelids felt as if they were being weighed down by anvils as she struggled to lift them and open her eyes.

It took her several tries before she succeeded. As she fought, she heard voices, felt the presence of bodies moving around her, surrounding her.

What was going on?

Oh, right, the invasion.

Two men in black, they'd broken into her house. One of them had grabbed her and hit her from behind.

Sam.

Sam!

That was when Riley finally opened her eyes. The first face she saw was Sam's.

"You're all right." She thought she shouted the words, but all she heard was a raspy whisper.

It was her own.

"Don't talk," Sam cautioned. He had his hands on her shoulders, restraining her as she tried to get up. "We're going to take you to the hospital."

There was a gurney beside the sofa. When had she laid down on the sofa? A gurney meant paramedics and an ambulance. Where had that come from? More importantly, why was it here? Her mother would have heart failure if she heard that an ambulance had been summoned for her.

"No, no hospital. I'm fine," she insisted. "Really."

The words carried no weight for Sam. "That's what you said before you passed out."

"I didn't pass out," she protested with as much indignation as she could muster under the circumstances.

"Okay," Sam allowed tersely. "You took a short nap. Either way, you sank to the floor and there's a nasty bump on the back of your head along with a nastier gash. You're bleeding. I want that gash looked at," he told her sternly.

"So look at it." She tried to raise her head to allow him to do just that, but the room began to spin. She fell back against the sofa again.

He saw the split second of weakness. "Damn it, woman, you're going to the hospital and that's that. I've had enough of a scare tonight. Do I make myself clear?" he demanded.

Riley stared at him as she tried to focus on what was going on. "The robbers?"

He assumed she was asking about the fact that the two were no longer in the room. "On their way to the precinct."

A lot of police personnel crowded into the room and most likely, beyond. Crime scene investigators? When had they gotten here? "How long was I out?"

"Too long," was all that Sam would tell her.

In reality, he'd spent a harrowing, endless fifteen minutes staring at her unconscious face, terrified and wondering if she would come to or wind up in a coma.

"You're not supposed to be here," she realized. When had he come back? And why? "You went home."

Sam shrugged, as if his appearance on the scene was of no great consequence. "I hung around for another forty-five minutes or so, thinking they might show up late. I was on my way out of your development when I passed a car with two guys sitting in the front. They looked like they had on black pullovers. It's too hot for black pullovers," he pointed out. "So I doubled back—just in case my hunch was right. And it was."

Riley began to nod, then stopped. The waves of pain crowding into her head made the motion impossible to complete.

"Good thing you did. I was already in bed, asleep. They caught me off guard."

Sam glanced toward the pile of books scattered on the floor near the door. "I'm guessing not entirely." He laughed, nodding toward the books. "First-class security alarm you have there."

"But it did the trick," she pointed out. "When they hit the books, the sound of them falling woke me up."

He should have stuck around, Sam admonished himself silently. If he had, they would have never gotten to her, never roughed her up. "Good thing."

She took a deep breath, letting it go again. It was over. They'd gotten the home invaders and she was incredibly relieved.

"You'd better go home to Lisa. I can handle the paperwork," she added in case that was on his mind.

Sam looked at her as if she was crazy. "You're not handling anything. What you're doing is going to the ER to get a once-over."

Riley huffed impatiently. "Wyatt, I already said that I'm—"

"Don't care what you said. I'm primary on this," he reminded her, "and what I say goes. Besides, I called your mother to tell her that we caught the robbers—"

Riley looked at him, horrified. "You didn't tell her I was hurt, did you?"

Wyatt made no attempt to hem and haw. "Your mother asked for details and I had to tell her. She's sending the chief to the hospital to see you so you'd better make an appearance there."

Riley closed her eyes, sighing. "I hate you," she said with no feeling.

"Yeah, I hate you, too," he told her with a grin. "Now get on the damn gurney before these paramedics grow old."

With another plaintive sigh—and help from Sam— Riley grudgingly got off the sofa and onto the gurney.

"I told you I was all right." A note of triumph registered in her voice as she turned toward Sam after receiving her discharge papers at the hospital some four hours later.

The woman was incorrigible. "They had to stitch up the gash in back of your head. Fifteen stitches is not 'all right,'" Sam pointed out, helping her off the hospital bed. He pulled back the curtain for her.

Her shrug was dismissive. "I had worse when Frank tackled me for taunting him when I was ten," she informed him.

Tonight was an education. If she'd ever doubted it,

she now had undeniable proof that word spread fast in the Cavanaugh network. She and Wyatt had barely gotten there when the first wave appeared. For a while, the hospital turned into a hotbed of activity as her siblings, stepbrothers, mother and stepfather came to the hospital to see how she was doing. It wasn't long before the rest of them turned up, as well. Only Zack's wife didn't come, but she had been pressed into service to remain with a sleeping Lisa so that Lila could come and see for herself that her youngest daughter was really all right the way she claimed.

"A hospital is a hell of a place to hold a family reunion," Riley had quipped at the height of the Cavanaugh influx. She felt absolutely awful about being the cause of concern for her mother and all the others who had abandoned their beds to come to the hospital in the middle of the night.

Satisfied that only "Riley's hard head," as Frank put it, was involved and that she would be all right, it had still taken a while for everyone to finally leave the premises.

"So how's your head?" Sam asked as he took her arm.

Riley hated to admit that she felt wobbly at first. But with each step, she became a little more sure-footed, a little stronger.

"Fine. Really," she underscored, knowing the last time she'd said that, it hadn't been true. But the bleeding had stopped and the wound sewn up, so by tomorrow, it would be business as usual. Except for maybe a headache.

Instead of going outside, Sam sat her down in the outer waiting area. For the time being, it was empty, but that was subject to change. "Clear enough to under-stand things?"

Why were they sitting here? She wanted to go home and put all this behind her. But she wasn't up to strug-gling with him, so she stayed where she was and humored him. "As long as you don't lapse into a foreign language, yes."

"Now that the cases are solved, I'm thinking of taking a couple of weeks off to spend some quality time with Lisa."

Why did he feel he had to sit her down to tell her this? "Good idea," she agreed. "I highly approve." But as she began to get up, he surprised her by gently pushing her back down.

"I'm not finished yet," he told her. "What do you think of taking some time off yourself—to spend with us?" Sam added when she made no response at first.

It took her only a second to roll the suggestion over in her head. Riley smiled. "I think that I'd like that."

Still, he made no attempt to get up.

"You know," Sam continued, "I'm really glad this is finally over—in large part thanks to you—and we can go back to the way things were."

He was buttering her up and it was working, she thought, suppressing a smile. "And what things are those?"

"Having you in my bed." Sam took a breath before continuing, taking her hands into his. "I'd never thought I'd hear myself saying this—hell, I never thought I'd catch myself feeling this way—but I've missed you, Riley. Missed being with you."

She felt herself melting. Still she wasn't sure where he was going with this. She only knew where she wished he'd go. "We were together every day."

"Not the way I wanted to be." Again, he paused and took a deep breath, as if that helped him get the rest of it out. He'd never been nervous around a woman before and it wasn't a feeling he welcomed. But this woman mattered more than any other ever had. "I love you, Riley."

She blinked. "Maybe my head isn't as fine as I thought," she confessed, her heart suddenly tap dancing in her chest. "I could have sworn I just heard you say you loved me."

"You did. I do." He watched the way surprise bloomed in her eyes. That made two of them. He never thought he would ever say those words to a woman. Love was something that happened to other men, not him. "I've suspected it for a while but wouldn't let myself think about it until tonight. Tonight, when I came in and that bastard had his gun on you, I thought I'd lost you. It was like having my gut ripped out with a jagged piece of glass."

Now there was an image to win over a woman's heart. "Very poetic," she said wryly.

"You want poetic?" he asked, then nodded. "I can try that. Might not be for a while, but I can try." His eyes held hers. "If you marry me."

She felt as if someone had just jumped on her stomach, making all the air come rushing out. "Did you just ask me to—"

"I did." He sat there, waiting for her answer.

He was serious, she thought. Actually serious. A myriad of fireflies suddenly materialized inside of her, filling her with light. She smiled at him. "You do drive a hard bargain, Wyatt, but I guess it'll be worth the trade."

"So is that a yes?"

An impish smile curved the corners of her mouth. "You need it spelled out?"

"Yes. Definitely. In big block letters."

She'd hire a skywriter if necessary. "All right. Yes, I'll marry you."

"Is that because you love me?"

Now there was a dumb question, she thought. "No, it's because I like doing penance. Yes, it's because I love you, idiot."

He finally rose, bringing her up with him. "Try it again without the idiot part."

Riley laughed as she entwined her arms around his neck. Her head didn't hurt anymore. Nothing hurt when there was this euphoria taking hold.

"Maybe later." She raised her lips to his. "Got something more important to do right now."

They both did.

* * * * *

Don't miss Marie Ferrarella's next romance,
DOCTORING THE SINGLE DAD,
available next month from Special Edition!

Rancher Ramsey Westmoreland's temporary cook is way too attractive for his liking. Little does he know Chloe Burton came to his ranch with another agenda entirely....

That man across the street had to be, without a doubt, the most handsome man she'd ever seen.

Chloe Burton's pulse beat rhythmically as he stopped to talk to another man in front of a feed store. He was tall, dark and every inch of sexy—from his Stetson to the well-worn leather boots on his feet. And from the way his jeans and Western shirt fit his broad muscular shoulders, it was quite obvious he had everything it took to separate the men from the boys. The combination was enough to corrupt any woman's mind and had her weakening even from a distance. Her body felt flushed. It was hot. Unsettled.

Over the past year the only male who had gotten her time and attention had been the e-mail. That was simply pathetic, especially since now she was practically drooling simply at the sight of a man. Even his stance—both hands in his jeans pockets, legs braced apart, was a pose she would carry to her dreams.

And he was smiling, evidently enjoying the conversation being exchanged. He had dimples, incredibly sexy dimples in not one but both cheeks.

"What are you staring at, Clo?"

Chloe nearly jumped. She'd forgotten she had a lunch date. She glanced over the table at her best friend from college, Lucia Conyers.

"Take a look at that man across the street in the blue shirt, Lucia. Will he not be perfect for Denver's first issue of *Simply Irresistible* or what?" Chloe asked with so much excitement she almost couldn't stand it.

She was the owner of *Simply Irresistible*, a magazine for today's up-and-coming woman. Their once-a-year Irresistible Man cover, which highlighted a man the magazine felt deserved the honor, had increased sales enough for Chloe to open a Denver office.

When Lucia didn't say anything but kept staring, Chloe's smile widened. "Well?"

Lucia glanced across the booth at her. "Since you asked, I'll tell you what I see. One of the Westmorelands—Ramsey Westmoreland. And yes, he'd be perfect for the cover, but he won't do it."

Chloe raised a brow. "He'd get paid for his services, of course."

Lucia laughed and shook her head. "Getting paid won't be the issue, Clo—Ramsey is one of the wealthiest sheep ranchers in this part of Colorado. But everyone knows what a private person he is. Trust me—he won't do it."

Chloe couldn't help but smile. The man was the epitome of what she was looking for in a magazine cover and she was determined that whatever it took, he would be it.

"Umm, I don't like that look on your face, Chloe. I've seen it before and know exactly what it means."

She watched as Ramsey Westmoreland entered the store with a swagger that made her almost breathless. She *would* be seeing him again.

Look for Silhouette Desire's
HOT WESTMORELAND NIGHTS
by Brenda Jackson,
available March 9 wherever books are sold.

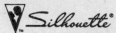

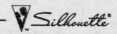

SPECIAL EDITION

FROM *USA TODAY* BESTSELLING AUTHOR
CHRISTINE RIMMER

A BRIDE FOR JERICHO BRAVO

Marnie Jones had long ago buried her wild-child impulses and opted to be "safe," romantically speaking. But one look at born rebel Jericho Bravo and she began to wonder if her thrill-seeking side was about to be revived. Because if ever there was a man worth taking a chance on, there he was, right within her grasp....

Available in March
wherever books are sold.

REQUEST YOUR FREE BOOKS!

2 FREE NOVELS
PLUS
2 FREE GIFTS!

Sparked by Danger, Fueled by Passion.

HARLEQUIN
Ambassadors

Want to share your passion for reading Harlequin® Books?

Become a Harlequin Ambassador!

Harlequin Ambassadors are a group of passionate and well-connected readers who are willing to share their joy of reading Harlequin® books with family and friends.

You'll be sent all the tools you need to spark great conversation, including free books!

All we ask is that you share the romance with your friends and family!

You'll also be invited to have a say in new book ideas and exchange opinions with women just like you!

To see if you qualify* to be a Harlequin Ambassador, please visit www.HarlequinAmbassadors.com.

Thank you for your participation.

BAP098PA